Which Witch is Which

J.L. Darling

For Amaya, Audrey, Alexis, & Marissa.
The four little witches that call me aunt and show me that love is unconditional magic.

"There is no magic when no one no longer believes"

-Hilda Lewis

"The Ship That Flew"

"Hey, Paisley! Wait up!"

Paisley Ireland turned to see her identical twin sister zooming across the lawn in front of Young Goodman Brown Middle School, her long brown hair streaming behind her.

"How come you didn't wait for me?" Bexley asked. "We always walk home together."

"I don't know, Bex. I'm in a hurry." Paisley glanced back at the girls Bexley had been talking to. She never had much to say to them. They always acted as if they were celebrities and all the people around them were the audience. But try to tell that to Bexley.

"Paisley," asked Bexley, "are you mad at me?"

Paisley grinned sarcastically at her sister. "Me, mad? Why would I be mad? You borrowed my wand without asking, you made me late for potions class, you got peanut butter in my hairbrush…why should I be mad?"

"But I always do things like that!" Bexley exclaimed.

Paisley threw up her hands. "Yes! Exactly!" Then started to laugh. "It's hard to stay mad at you—it's not any of those things, really. I just get bored around those girls and I have tons of homework, that's all."

"Plus, you have to help me with my spells," Bexley added.

"Yes, your highness." Paisley sighed. It would be a tight squeeze, finishing all her stuff and coaching Bexley too, but she didn't want to let her sister down.

The girls started down the tree-lined street toward home.

"Did you see Olive Foster in gym class today?" Bexley asked. "She's not graceful at all or coordinated. It's like she was born with two left feet."

"Bexley," Paisley said, "you shouldn't talk about other people."

"Oh, I know," Bexley insisted. "But the dance would look so much better without her."

"Bexley," Paisley groaned.

"Well, she was ruining our class," complained Bexley. "Dance is supposed to be beautiful and graceful, and she was crashing around like a clumsy ostrich. It's tough on the kids with real talent."

"Like Ms. Bexley Ireland?" Paisley teased.

"Absolutely. Maybe I'll be a famous dancer someday. I'm going to practice until I'm the best dancer at Young Goodman Brown."

"Bexley," Paisley said suddenly. "I have great news!"

"Don't tell me we're finally getting our own cell phones!"

Paisley laughed. "Even better. Professor Martin is going to let us start an online magazine for the middle school. I asked him today. And he put me in charge! You could write a gossip column or something!"

"Lola Van Doren would be better at that. She knows every drop of tea that's spilled at Young Goodman Brown Middle practically before it happens. She even knows about the seventh and eighth graders."

"How about fashion, or reality TV?"

Bexley looked bored and shook her head no.

"You mean-you don't want to write for it?" Paisley was shocked. She and Bexley always did things together. They dressed alike, they shared a room, they watched the same shows on TV, they went shopping together—they were inseparable.

"I just don't think I'll have time, that's all," Bexley said casually.

Paisley tried not to feel disappointed. But it would feel awfully strange to do something so important without Bexley involved. "Well, I think the magazine will be great," she said, "but I know you're busy."

"Okay, big sister."

Paisley smiled. It was one of their favorite jokes. She was only seven minutes older than Bexley, but that still made her the big sister. She always felt like the responsible older sister. She had to remind Bexley to do practically everything, help her with spells, and pick up after her. Where would Bexley be without her?

The girls reached their corner, turned down the driveway to their big cape house, and let themselves in through the kitchen door. Usually, they were the first ones home. Both their parents worked. Their mother, being a green witch, was a herbologist at a local greenhouse that specialized in both native and exotic plants. Their father was a Bloodhound for the D.M.M.—Department of Magical Mischief—there was always some witch trying to bend the rules of magic. Their older brother, Reed, was a freshman at Nathaniel Hawthorne High. Sometimes he stayed after school for soccer practice. But just at that moment he came in, slamming the kitchen door behind him and throwing his backpack on the floor.

“What’s wrong with you?” asked Bexley as Reed rummaged angrily through the refrigerator.

“None of your business,” he snapped.

Paisley and Bexley rolled their eyes. He had turned into a real jerk since the first day he started high school.

The twins sat down at the kitchen table with a carton of fresh strawberries while Reed slumped down in a chair with a plate in his hand. He pulled out his wand and pointed to the plate. A giant slice of chocolate cake with peanut butter frosting appeared. “That slaps,” he said through a mouth full of peanut butter frosting.

“Ew, do you have to be so gross?” Paisley asked with a scrunched-up face.

“You’re just jealous you can’t use magic yet, so you have to eat whatever mom buys for the house. Cool outfits by the way,” he said, smirking, as he looked from one sister to the other.

"What's the matter with them?" Paisley wanted to know.

"Nothing," Reed said, "if you like having double vision. Don't you think you're a little old to be dressing the same?"

"No," Bexley said.

"No wonder nobody can tell you apart."

"They can too!" Bexley said. But Paisley kept quiet. Kids at school were always staring at her saying, "Uh…Bexley?" Paisley looked across the table at Bexley. It was like looking into a mirror. She saw her own chocolate brown hair pulled pack into a ponytail, her emerald-green eyes and long lashes, and even the dimple in her left cheek. She also saw the same white t-shirt, and she knew that under the table were the denim skirt and white Vans she was wearing. But so, what? Dressing alike was part of the fun of being a twin.

"It would take a bloodhound witch to know which one of you was which," mumbled Reed, his mouth full of cake.

"Okay, okay, we get the point," said Paisley. "But we like dressing alike."

Reed started to say something else, but the phone rang and he and Bexley both dashed for it, knocking over their chairs. Bexley got there first.

"Hello?" Paisley could hear her say breathlessly. "Oh, hi." Bexley cradled the phone against her ear and walked into the dining room.

"That was Jett Andrews," Bexley announced, strolling back into the kitchen. She sounded as though she'd been talking to a member of the royal family.

"Who cares?" Reed said. Then he got up and strutted out of the kitchen.

Paisley knew all about Jett Andrews. She had the biggest wardrobe in Salem. Her father was the Grand High Witch, which meant he was rich and bought her everything she wanted. Bexley had been spending a lot of time with her lately, although Paisley couldn't understand why.

"She's in the Black Cats Club," Bexley told her sister.

"What's that?" Paisley asked. "Did Jett's father turn a bunch of children into black cats for Jett to play with?"

"This is nothing to joke about," Bexley declared in a superior tone. "It's called the Black Cats Club because black cats are beautiful and special, and everyone likes them." Her sister gave her a look like you've got to be kidding me. "Well, witches like them. Humbums are afraid of them. Did you know Humbums believe that if a black cat crosses their path, it's bad luck and they roll up their pant legs to prevent the bad luck. Crazy right?" Her sister still did not look impressed. "Anyway, hardly any sixth graders get to join. But Jett's in, and Alexis Jacobs too. They're so lucky. Of course, Audrey Parker is Jett's cousin."

"And who's Audrey Parker?" Paisley asked sounding bored.

Bexley sighed. "Don't you know anything? Audrey Parker is only the prettiest, most popular witch in eighth grade. She's the president of the club."

Paisley leaned forward. "Listen, if you're really so up on everything." She said, seriously, "you ought to write for the magazine."

"No!" Bexley said. "And please don't ask me again, Paisley."

"Sorry." Paisley changed the subject. "Let's go start our homework.

Okay?"

"You go ahead," Bexley told her. "I want to practice dance." Her green eyes began to sparkle. "Especially those spins the dancers make at the end when everyone applauds and throws flowers." Bexley darted out of the kitchen, leaving a pile of strawberry stems on the table.

Typical Bexley, Paisley thought. Paisley got an antibacterial wipe and quickly wiped up the table. Then she headed upstairs to her bedroom, dropped her books on her bed and flopped down after them. She gazed around the room. It was pretty, Paisley thought, but maybe a little babyish. The walls were ballet slipper pink with silver and gold stars, the rug was also pink, and she and Bexley each had matching white comforters and pink pillows on their beds. Pink and white, pink and white. Paisley didn't even like pink very much. It was Bexley who chose it. And Bexley 's side of the room was an unbelievable mess. Clothes, magazines, socks, chewing gum wrappers, jewelry-junk was spilling out everywhere. Paisley wasn't sure how her twin would be able to unearth her bed that night.

With a sigh Paisley settled down at her desk and launched into her homework. She kept on going until just before dinnertime.

Bexley had to be ordered up from the basement to help make the salad. She kept complaining that dance was a lot more important than chores, and then disappeared again. She came to dinner still dressed in her leotard.

"What's this?" Mr. Ireland asked.

"Oh, Daddy," exclaimed Bexley, "we're taking dance in gym, and I love it."

"Maybe you girls would like to take dance at Madame Pappenheimer's School of Dance," Mrs. Ireland suggested.

"Are you serious," Bexley shrieked.

Mrs. Ireland laughed. "Of course, I am. I'll call the studio first thing tomorrow."

Over dessert Paisley told her parents and Reed about getting permission to start an online magazine. "And you know what? It will be the first middle school magazine ever," she finished.

"That's great!" her mother said.

"Tomorrow I'm going to ask Marissa Fairchild and Amaya-Jane Farrington to be on it," Paisley exclaimed. "I can't wait."

Bexley made a face. "All you need is Isaac Wardwell, and you can call it the "Nerdpaper," she said. "I mean, honestly. Marissa Fairchild does her homework at recess, and she wears such boring clothes and don't get me started on Amaya—"

"Bexley! You are unbelievable! Marissa and Amaya are a lot smarter and more interesting than the snobby girls you think are so great. And what gives you the right to say that—you don't even want to be on the magazine!" Paisley exclaimed.

There was a surprised silence. Their parents looked at each other stunned at their daughter's behavior.

"I am much too busy," Bexley said in her most haughty voice.

"You are a wicked-wicked Elphaba, Bexley!" Paisley said.

"And you're a goody-goody Glinda," said Bexley as she stuck out her tongue at her sister.

"Bexley Ireland, we did not raise you to talk about other people like that," her father said.

"Yes, daddy," she said as she looked down at the table.

"Well, Flotsam and Jetsam actually have separate interests," Reed said, smirking. "Or anyway, one of them does."

"I have plenty of things on my mind, too," Bexley declared. "You'll see."

Paisley had a feeling Bexley was telling the truth. There was something on her mind. And it had nothing whatsoever to do with her twin sister. Somehow, for no good reason, that really bothered her.

Paisley climbed into bed that night feeling very tired, but she couldn't fall asleep. She still couldn't believe that Bexley would rather spend time with snobby, boring girls like Jett Andrews. Well, she could only hope that Bexley would change her mind. After all, they were twins. And no matter what Reed or anybody else says, twins belong together.

Two

The next morning Paisley decided she wouldn't say a single word to Bexley about the magazine. She'd just talk to Marissa and Amaya and get it started. Then, when the magazine turned out amazing, Bexley would definitely want to be in on it.

Bexley seemed to be in just as much of a hurry to get to school as Paisley was. After a quick breakfast the twins picked up their identical blue backpacks and dashed out the kitchen door. "Let's take the shortcut past the Good house," Paisley said. "Maybe I'll be able to catch Amaya and Marissa before class."

"Not a chance," said Bexley. "We will just have to run."

By the time they reached school, the grounds were already crawling with kids. Young Goodman Brown Middle was much bigger than the elementary school. Its stone walls sprawled out in every direction on acres of lush green lawn. The twins loved it there, although finding a friend before homeroom was a definite challenge.

"Hi, brownie!" a voice suddenly called.

Both girls spun around.

Sebastian Bradbury was strolling past them with a big grin on his face. He was a really cute seventh grader from one of the richest families in town. Unfortunately, he thought he was the most important person in the world, and he often acted like a bully and a jerk, at least in Paisley's opinion.

This was a perfect example. Sebastian thought it was hilarious to call them both "brownie." He said it was much easier than trying to tell them apart. Some of the other kids had even started doing it too. Paisley could just imagine what Reed would say if he ever found out.

"I wish he'd stop that," Paisley muttered, then she noticed that Bexley was paying no attention. She was smiling and staring dreamily after Sebastian as though he were Tom Holland or something.

"Paisley," she whispered, "I think Sebastian likes me!"

Paisley was dumbfounded. "I thought you hated boys!" she exclaimed. "All summer long you kept saying how gross they were."

"That was ages ago," Bexley said airily. Suddenly she started jumping up and down and waving. "There they are," she cried. Jett Andrews and Alexis Jacobs were sitting on the school steps waving back. "I've got to talk to them," she told Paisley, and darted across the lawn.

Paisley took two steps after Bexley and stopped in her tracks. She had almost forgotten the magazine! It was very easy to get swept along by Bexley Ireland. But not this time. She had other things on her mind. Paisley hurried off to find Amaya and Marissa.

She felt as though she had covered every inch of the school, when suddenly she saw them—just as the homeroom bell started to ring. "Oh," Paisley cried, "I've got something exciting to tell you! And there's no time."

Marissa's eyes lit up. "Let's meet for lunch," she said.

Paisley hesitated. She and Bexley usually sat together in the cafeteria. But, she decided, Marissa and Amaya could join them. With a little luck, Bexley might decide she liked them.

At lunchtime Paisley and Bexley dashed to the cafeteria and grabbed their usual table. They were just about to sit down, when they both gasped, "Oh, I forgot!" They looked at each other.

"Jett and Alexis asked me to sit with them today," Bexley explained. "I guess you could come along if you really wanted to, but…" Her voice trailed off.

"I wanted to talk to Marissa and Amaya anyway," Paisley said quickly. "See you," she called as she watched her brunette twin disappear through the crowded cafeteria. It was weird, Paisley thought. She would a million times rather talk to

Marissa and Amaya than sit with those other girls, but she still felt as though she were missing out on something.

"Paisley! Here you are," Amaya said breathlessly. Marissa was at her side. "We stood in that lunch line forever."

"What did you want to tell us?" Marissa asked as they sat down.

Suddenly Paisley felt nervous. Suppose Marissa and Amaya thought her idea was stupid, too? She took a deep breath. "I was thinking it would be fun to start a middle school online magazine. It's okay with Professor Martin. I thought we could have interviews and stories about class events—"

Amaya's eyes were sparkling. "I just love advice columns and inquiring reporters who go around asking kids' stuff like "What do you think about dating in middle school?"

Marissa interrupted. "And a gossip column; that's a must. And sports, and movie reviews, and a poetry corner—am I getting carried away?"

“I guess you like the idea.” Paisley laughed. “Let’s start brainstorming.”

All three girls opened their notebooks and were scribbling away when Lola Van Doren suddenly plunked herself down next to Paisley.

Paisley groaned inwardly. Lola Van Doren lived two doors away from the Irelands and was the snobbiest person in the world. Lola also had the biggest mouth in Salem. Telling her a secret was like posting it on your public snapchat story.

“Guess what?” Lola said, looking very smug. She glanced at the girls’ notebooks as they snapped them shut. “They’re going to fire Faulkner.”

“Professor Faulkner? Now? At the beginning of the year?” asked Marissa.

Professor Faulkner, the head of the history department, was the oldest teacher in the school, and one of the nicest.

“I don’t know,” replied Lola. “But he must have done something horrendous. Do you know what else? Katarina

Black was grounded for a week for staying out really late with a high school boy."

"Lola," Paisley demanded, "how do you know what the eighth graders are doing?"

Lola looked mysterious. "I hear things," she said. She stood up. "See you."

"OMG," Amaya said breathlessly, "a high school boy."

"Yeah," Paisley said. Even if Lola's stories weren't always a hundred percent accurate, she couldn't wait to tell Bexley.

On the other side of the cafeteria Bexley was sitting with Alexis, Jett, Audrey Parker and three seventh graders, Margot Hutchins, Blair Scott, and Fiona Burroughs. Bexley had never been more excited in her life. She felt as though an enormous spotlight were shining on her table. Kids kept looking their way, and she had lost count of the cute boys who had waved hello. She could hardly blame them. Every girl at the table was fabulous—looking and dressed in great clothes.

Bexley knew she could hold her own in the looks department. With silky chocolate, brown hair, emerald-green eyes, and perfect features, there was no doubt about it. But the other girls at the table had one thing in common that she didn't share—they were all members of the Black Cats Club.

More than anything in the world, Bexley wanted to belong to the Black Cats Club. And she was more determined than ever to find a way in. "So…what do you do at your meetings?" Bexley asked.

"Well," Jett drawled, tossing her long raven-black hair behind her shoulders, "I guess we can tell you." She leaned across the table and lowered her voice. "A lot of times we talk about people, like who's going out with who and who's breaking up with who."

"Oh," said Bexley, feeling slightly disappointed.

Alexis took over. “And,” she whispered dramatically, her blue eyes flashing, “we talk about boys.”

Bexley straightened up. “Oh,” she said with a knowing smile.

“The thing is,” Audrey went on, “we’re always a group. We sit together at lunch. We hang out together after school. Lots of times we go to the Bit Bar.”

The Bit Bar! That was where the high school kids hung out. Bexley had never been there without her parents. This was getting better and better.

“We plan things, too,” Audrey added. “Like, this year we decided neon pink is our favorite color, so we all bought neon pink stuff to wear.”

Bexley checked the girls’ clothes. They were wearing an awful lot of neon pink.

“We pay dues every week,” Jett said, “to cover expenses—like food for sleepovers. This Friday we’re going to

Flying Saucer Pizza Company. We've got enough money for four large pizzas."

"Four?" repeated Bexley. They must be big eaters.

"There are twelve of us in the club," Alexis said. "And some boys might drop by our table."

"We don't want the club to get any bigger," Audrey put in. "It's exclusive."

Bexley felt her hopes begin to fade.

"But," Jett said meaningfully, "a few new Black Cats—Like Alexis and me—get in every year to replace the kids who graduate or move away."

Bexley held her breath. "Is there room for anyone else?" she barely managed to ask.

"Maybe," replied Audrey, looking straight at her. That was all Bexley needed to hear. When Bexley Ireland wanted something, there was no "maybe." There was only "yes."

Three

The next morning Paisley woke up with a start. A horrible groan was coming from her sister's bed.

"Bexley!" she whispered. "What is it?"

"Ohhh," Bexley moaned. "I didn't finish half my homework. All of those rotten spells. Paisley, I've just got to copy yours."

"Bexley, Professor Bishop would hex us if she found out. And I don't want to get into trouble. I'll help you with the spells during homeroom, okay?"

Bexley made a face. "All right, Miss Perfect." She struggled to get out of bed and stood in front of the closet. "You know," she told Paisley, "We don't own nearly enough neon pink. Why don't we have more neon pink clothes?"

Paisley shrugged. “Because we don’t want to look like we’re from the 90’s?”

Bexley giggled. She finally picked out jeans, a white t-shirt, and her neon pink zip up sweatshirt.

Paisley quickly pulled on the same outfit.

“Paisley,” Bexley asked a minute later, “I can’t find my Jordans. Have you seen them?”

Paisley shook her head.

“Can I borrow yours then?”

Paisley was just sliding her feet into her new sneakers. “I’ve worn my Jordans only twice,” she explained. “And they look so good with my jeans. Can’t you wear something else?” How about your Uggs?”

“Paisley, no one wears Uggs anymore. Please let me borrow your Jordans. Just this once?”

“Oh, all right.” Paisley sighed. “Try to keep them clean though. And while we’re on the subject, why don’t we clean out this place after school?” She nodded toward Bexley’s side of the room. “Sebastian Bradbury could be under that mess, and you wouldn’t even know it.”

“I wish.” Bexley giggled. “Okay, let’s. And thanks. Jeez, what would I do without you?”

“I don’t know,” Paisley said seriously.

On the way to school Paisley suddenly remembered Lola Van Doren and her stories. “Hey,” she exclaimed, “you know what Lola told me yesterday? They’re going to fire Professor Faulkner.”

“You’re kidding me! He’s been around forever.”

“No, honest. You know what else? Katarina Black was grounded for staying out late with a high school boy!”

“I know,” Bexley said disdainfully. “She got kicked out of the Black Cats Club for that.”

“For that?” Paisley was amazed. “I bet half the girls in the club are dying to go out with a high school boy!”

"That was probably just the last straw," Bexley said as though she were telling a major secret. "She and Audrey weren't getting along very well. Besides, I heard this boy kept putting the Black Cats down."

Paisley didn't answer. No matter what they talked about lately, the conversation always seemed to get around to the Black Cats. Bexley seemed to think it was the world's most fascinating topic. But if Paisley heard one more word about them, she was going to scream. They were about five minutes from school. Only one other thing might hold Bexley's attention that long. She switched the subject to dance.

That did the trick. Bexley chattered away about how much she loved to dance and how good she was, right up and into homeroom.

After classes Paisley went to her usual spot on the lawn to wait for Bexley. She was actually looking forward to cleaning the bedroom when they got home, even if the mess wasn't hers. The room wouldn't look like a junkyard for a change, plus she'd have the whole afternoon with Bexley.

But where was she? The school grounds were emptying out. Bexley was usually late, but this was ridiculous. Finally, the truth hit her. Bexley was not going to show up. She had been waiting for almost a half hour. And Bexley hadn't even cared enough to let her know she wasn't coming. She didn't know who made her feel worse—herself, for waiting forever, or Bexley, for having no consideration at all. Paisley picked up her backpack and headed for home.

Bexley, meanwhile, was strolling with Jett Andrews toward the Bit Bar. She had seen Jett after the last class of the day, and Jett had invited her to go with some of the Black Cats As soon as Bexley heard that, she had forgotten everything else, including her sister. When they reached the Bit Bar, Jett led her to a table where Margot Hutchins and Alexis Jacobs were sitting with Audrey Parker. As soon as they saw her, the girls looked at one another and grinned as though they knew a huge secret. Bexley's heart began to pound.

Even before their order came, Audrey said in a serious tone, "Bexley, we wanted to meet you here for a very important reason."

Bexley's heart increased its pace. "Yes?" she said breathlessly.

"We have room for two more girls in the Black Cats Club," Audrey went on. "We ask only very special people, you know, girls who can keep up the image of the club. And—' she paused dramatically. "We think you're Black Cat material."

Bexley's heart was really racing now.

"Do you know about the pledge tasks?" Audrey asked.

"Pledge tasks?" Bexley asked.

"They're our initiation. After we see how you do your pledge tasks, we vote on whether to let you into the club."

Bexley sat up a little straighter. "What do you want me to do?"

“Well,” said Jett, “you have three tasks. First you have to hide Professor Proctor’s wand at the beginning of History and get it back into her bag by the end of class—without her seeing you.”

“The Proctor’s wand?” Bexley gasped. “She can’t do anything without that. It’s practically glued to her hands.” Professor Proctor had been at the school almost as long as Professor Faulkner, and every day—without fail—she carefully penciled in her eyebrows in two perfect half-moons above her eyes. Her wand was like her security blanket. Bexley thought of something else. “Hey,” she squealed, “she never lets anybody out of their seats!”

“That’s right!” Jett grinned at Bexley. “Second, you have to stand outside the girls’ room between classes and tell at least three girls that the bathroom floor is flooded so they’re supposed to use the boys’ room. And you actually have to get three girls to go into the boys’ room.”

“Oh, no,” Bexley shrieked.

"And last, you have to come to school one day looking so different from Paisley that no one would know you're twins."

"How am I going to do that?" Plastic Surgery?"

"We didn't say it would be easy," Jett answered. "Now, remember, the pledge tasks are top secret. You can't tell anyone why you're doing them. Not a soul. And that includes your sister."

Bexley thought of something. "So, Paisley can't tell me her tasks either—"

"Paisley?" Audrey looked dumbfounded. "What do you mean?"

"Well, you said two new members. She's going to be the other one, isn't she?"

"The other new member," Audrey said, "is, Penelope Duncan that eighth grader who just moved here. We weren't planning to ask Paisley. She's nice and all. But she's not right for the Black Cats."

Bexley felt shocked. She wanted to stick up for her sister, but what could she say? She and Paisley were different, very different. It was hard to see Paisley fitting in with the Black Cats. Audrey definitely had a point.

The only problem was Paisley. She might not see it that way at all. Bexley really didn't want to hurt her sisters' feelings, but there was no way she would turn down the chance to join the most amazing club in school. She'd been dreaming of it ever since she first heard of the Black Cats.

Well, thought Bexley, she had promised to do her pledge tasks without Paisley finding out. Suppose she just didn't say anything at all about the Black Cats Club—not even that she had been asked to join? Then she could still become a member, and Paisley's feeling wouldn't be hurt—or, at least, not right away. Later, when she was in, Bexley would probably think of a way to tell her and fix everything.

That's it, Bexley thought. I'll just keep the whole thing a secret.

But it wasn't going to be easy. Not at all. How was she going to keep a secret from her own twin sister? Bexley and Paisley had never kept secrets from each other.

Four

"Bexley, where were you today?" Paisley demanded as soon as her sister set foot in the house.

Bexley clapped her hand over her mouth. "Oh, I forgot! I was with the—with Jett Andrews," she said quickly. "I ran into her after school, and she asked me to go to the Bit Bar." This was all true.

"I waited for you for ages. Don't you remember? We were going to clean our room—meaning your half. You could have told me."

"I know. I'm truly sorry. It just popped out of my head. Look"—Bexley was in a hurry to change the subject— "I bought us these neon pink belts today." She pulled a package from her book bag. "We can wear them tomorrow. See?" She held the belts up.

Paisley felt anger fade away, Bexley hadn't really forgotten her completely—although she had forgotten she didn't like pink. "That was nice of you, Bex. I guess you can't help being a scatterbrain. Although," she couldn't help adding, "you could try to remember these things."

"Next time I'll remember, promise. Hey, did you finish cleaning the room?"

Paisley could not believe her sister. "Are you kidding?"

"I just thought, since you weren't doing anything anyway… I know it's my mess, but it doesn't bother me…"

Paisley started to giggle. Maybe that was how Bexley always got around her. She was so oblivious, it was funny.

"I did not touch one candy wrapper," Paisley said. "But I'll clean up with you now."

"Great! Let's use a little magic and we will have this room cleaned in no time!" said Bexley.

"No way," Paisley said crossing her arms. "You know the rules. We can't start using magic until we are thirteen. And besides you know we aren't supposed to use magic for chores."

"I know. I know. I just don't understand what's the point of being a witch if we can't use our magic. So frustrating." Said Bexley looking around the room.

"We'd better get started," said Paisley.

"Ok! But first we've just got to see how the belts look with our black jumpers, and there's a good movie on…"

As they went up the stairs, Paisley thought to herself, *we won't get much done, but we'll have a good time. Things are getting back to normal again.*

Bexley woke up the next morning with butterflies in her stomach. Today was the day. She had to tackle pledge task number one—Professor Proctor's wand. It was going to be hard enough to steal it away from her in the first place, but having to get it back into her bag, during the same class…wow! And what if Professor Proctor caught her? The

Proctor might be soft, but she got tough over anything that even hinted of dishonesty. A "breach of trust" she called it. Bexley could just see herself being dragged to the principal with Professor Proctor screaming, "Expel the thief!"

But this kind of thinking would get her nowhere. *I will not get caught*, she said to herself. *I will get the wand. I will be a Black Cat!*

When she got to school, Jett and Alexis were waiting for her. "Are you ready?" Jett asked.

"As ready as I'll ever be. I've got a plan."

"Oh, I can't wait!" cried Jett. She had Professor Proctor with Bexley.

"Good," replied Bexley, "because I'm going to need you."

"Wait, Jett can't help you with a pledge task," said Alexis. "Pledge tasks have to be done on your own."

"It's just one teeny—weeny thing. I need Jett to create just one little distraction. I'll do everything else all by myself."

“What sort of distraction do you want?”

“Could you get the Proctor talking?” Bexley asked. “Just ask her something about The Salem Witch Trials. You know how she is on that subject.”

“Doesn’t everybody?” Jett grinned. “Okay.”

By the time the girls got to their History of Salem class, Professor Proctor was already in the classroom, eyebrows as firmly in place, as the wand in her hand. Bexley grimaced and glanced at Jett. She prayed that the wand would at least be lying on the teacher’s desk.

When most of the students were seated, Professor Proctor pointed the wand toward the board. “Are there any questions about last night’s homework?” she asked the class.

Bexley nodded to Jett. This was it.

Jett’s hand shot up.

“Yes, Jett?”

"I was wondering if you could tell us again about your grandfather John Proctor, and how his child survived the witch trials."

"My tenth great grandfather," Professor Proctor corrected her. She smoothed her eyebrows. "Why, yes, Jett. John Proctor was accused of witchcraft and was jailed, of course, and my experiences are relevant to…" She set the wand down on her desk and walked over to Jett. Bexley breathed a sigh of relief.

"Let's see," Professor Proctor continued, deep in thought.

Bexley raised her hand and waved it frantically. "May I leave the room?"

"I'm sure you can wait, dear. A little control, you know. We witches learned that on the front lines of the trials." Professor Proctor didn't want anyone to miss a single second of her class.

Bexley tried to look embarrassed. “It’s an emergency,” she said with a little tear in her voice.

Professor Proctor waved her out and focused on Jett again.

Bexley made a dash for the door, counted out two minutes, and slid back into the classroom. Professor Proctor was still talking away. As Bexley passed the teacher’s desk, she casually picked up the wand, holding it behind her back as she made her way to her seat. A few snickers came from the back of the classroom.

Professor Proctor never stopped talking. Each time it seemed there wasn’t a single thing left to say about The Salem Witch Trials, someone would come up with one more question. The only problem was that most of the time Professor Proctor was looking right at Bexley—and somehow Bexley had to get the wand back into Professor Proctor’s bag. The bell was going to ring in five minutes.

Professor Proctor finished a point and returned to her desk. Her right hand reached absently for her wand.

Bexley's stomach tied itself into a knot.

Professor Proctor looked through the papers on her desk. "Dear me," she said. "Where's my…?"

Bexley and Jett stared at each other.

"Class, has anybody seen my wand?" Professor Proctor asked.

Nobody said a word.

There were three minutes left until the bell rang.

"Professor Proctor?" Across the room a hand waved wildly. It belonged to Isaac Wardwell, usually one of the quieter kids.

"Yes, Isaac?"

"I don't know where your wand is," he said. His eyes strayed to Bexley. "But can you show us how the witches stood at attention, you know, eyes forward like during a drill?"

Professor Proctor's frown disappeared. She stiffened up, marched across the room, saluted Isaac, and stared ahead. When Professor Proctor's back was turned, Bexley rose from her seat. She tiptoed up and crouched down behind the big desk. Professor Proctor's ancient briefcase was on the floor. Bexley began to fumble with the clasp. She could hear Isaac saying, "Do you think it was scary being a witch during that time?" The bag suddenly opened with a snap like a rifle shot. At the same time the bell rang, and Bexley shoved the wand in. She stood up.

"Why, yes, Isaac! It was the most terrifying time for a witch, if it wasn't for our ancestors, witches in Salem would still be in hiding and fearful for their lives. Now, thanks to them, we can co-exist amongst the Humbums. They have made rules to govern our magic because they are still afraid of us, but we no longer have to be afraid of them," Professor Proctor was saying as she caught sight of Bexley. "My, you're in a hurry today, dear. Let's not forget your homework." Then it all came back to her. “My wand…I’m sorry, children. No homework tonight.”

A loud cheer went up as everyone hurried out. Professor Proctor was searching all over her desk, trying to find her wand, muttering, “I could swear…” Isaac was in front of Bexley.

“Not bad, Isaac,” she called, and watched his ears turn tomato-red.

As soon as she was in the hallway, Bexley turned to Jett. “Phew!” she exclaimed. “I did it!”

“And” Jett added, “you got us out of a night’s homework, too!”

Bexley waited until Friday to tackle her second pledge task. She didn’t dare ask Jett to help her on this one. She’d simply have to stake out the girls’ room and hope she’d get lucky. She figured the second-floor bathroom was her best bet.

Not many eighth graders used it. They'd be hardest to trick—they were old enough to use magic.

As soon as the bell rang after third period, Bexley stationed herself on the second floor and put on a serious expression. Alexis and Audrey were standing across the hall from the girls' room so they wouldn't miss anything.

The hallway was already swarming with kids, and right away two eighth graders headed for the girls' room door.

Darn, I was hoping for sixth graders. Oh well, here I go, she thought to herself. Bexley stepped in front of them. "Sorry," she said. "The girl's room is flooded. No one's allowed in."

"Who're you?" demanded one of the girls.

"The bathroom monitor," Bexley said crisply. "You're supposed to use the boys' room across the hall. Just until the caretaker finishes."

The girls looked at each other. "Come on," said the other one, shrugging. "We'll go to the first floor."

The first floor! Bexley heart sank. She hadn't thought about the other girls' room. What if everyone remembered it? She'd be humiliated.

The eighth graders were three feet away when Olive Foster stepped up.

"You can't go in there." Bexley barred the way. "It's an absolute lake. The Eyebrows told me to keep everybody out while the caretaker fixes the leak."

"Well, what am I supposed to do?" Olive puffed.

"Use the boys' room." Bexley pointed across the hall.

Olive looked mortified.

"There are only two and a half minutes left before fourth period," Bexley warned her. She was counting the seconds.

Olive's face fell. "Okay."

Bexley watched nervously as Olive crossed the hall and hesitated under the sign that said BOYS. Cautiously she pushed the door open, poked her head in, and listened. Then she went inside, the door swinging shut behind her.

She was out in one second. “There are boys in there,” she announced indignantly, and fled down the hall.

“That has to count,” Bexley called to Audrey. “She went all the way in.”

Audrey was laughing so hard she couldn’t answer, so Bexley knew she had scored.

One down, two to go.

Bexley was feeling pretty smug until she saw who was headed for the bathroom next—Marissa, Amaya, and Paisley. Bexley nearly fell over. Now what should she do? There was no way she was going to embarrass her own sister. Bexley decided to let Paisley speak first.

“Hi, Bexley!” Paisley said. “What are you doing?”

“Oh, waiting for Jett,” Bexley said quickly.

“Come on, Paisley,” Marissa said. “The bell’s going to ring.”

“See you later.” Paisley disappeared into the girls’ room

Bexley watched glumly. Out of the corner of her eye she saw Audrey shaking her head. What if she thought Bexley wasn't fit to be a Black Cat?

But Bexley didn't have time to worry. Two more girls were coming her way. Eighth graders by the looks of them. Too bad. They were her only chance.

"Sorry," Bexley said in a firm voice. "Bathrooms flooded. You'll have to use the boys' room."

The taller girl looked suspicious. "I just saw someone go in."

The seconds were ticking away. Bexley groped for an answer. "Oh, sure…she's a water witch. She's going to help control the leak."

"Water witch?"

"They're not very active, but they're great in emergencies. Anyway, I'm the bathroom monitor and I'm supposed to send you to the boys' room."

The second girl started to laugh. “Come on, Jemma,” she said. “I’ve always wanted to see inside the boys’ bathroom!”

A smile spread across Jemma’s face. “YOLO!”

Bexley held her breath. As soon as the door to the boy’s room closed behind the girls she heard screams and shouts she didn't wait a second longer she and Audrey and Alexis took off down the hall laughing like crazy.

Bexley decided to wait until Monday to tackle her last pledge task. This was the very worst one. Looking different from her identical twin would be hard enough but doing it without telling Paisley seemed nearly impossible. Still, there had to be a way. She started to think. Paisley always puts on the same outfit her sister did. But maybe this time, Bexley thought, she could arrange things so that Paisley had to get dressed first. And maybe, she thought, the ideas coming faster now, she could convince Reed to use a glamour spell on her to make her look different from Paisley.

On Monday morning, according to plan, Bexley stayed in bed while her sister stood in front of the closet. "What should we wear today?" Paisley asked.

Bexley yawned. "You got me." She rolled over and pretended to doze off.

"Come on, Bex. Make up your mind," Paisley said.

Bexley kept her eyes closed and her breathing even.

Paisley looked at her twin. "OK," she said. "Our black rompers."

Through her long lashes Bexley saw Paisley lay out both outfits, dress quickly, and start downstairs. "Pumpkin potion pancakes, Bex?" she called over her shoulder.

In two minutes, Bexley was out of bed putting on an entirely different outfit. She chose her black skirt and neon pink sweater and ran into Reeds room, where he was still laying under his covers. “Reed, wake up, hurry!” she said as she shook the mound under the plaid comforter.

“What?” Reed groaned not moving.

“I need you to do a glamour spell on me before I leave for school. I’ll clean your room,” she said.

“Clean my room for two weeks and we have a deal,” Reed said poking his head from under the covers.

“Fine,” Bexley groaned. “I’ll clean your room for two weeks. Just get up, hurry, I’m running out of time.”

Reed reached for his wand on the nightstand and sat up in bed. “Ok, and what would you like to look like?” he asked as he pointed his wand at Bexley’s face.

“I need to look different than Paisley. So, maybe some highlights, curls and a little makeup. Just think Arianna Grande.”

Reed laughed but said, “coming right up,”

Bexley checked the time. She and Paisley would have to leave for school in less than 10 minutes. Perfect—as long as Paisley didn't make a fuss.

Hopefully Reed understood the assignment and didn’t make her look like JoJo Siwa, Bexley thought to herself as she took a deep breath and stepped in front of the mirror. Wow, the change was subtle, yet she looked so much different. She reached her hand up and smoothed the caramel highlights that now framed her heart shaped face. Her lashes were longer and fuller making her emerald-green eyes pop, and there was a hint of color in her cheeks. Not bad, Reed! She thought as she finished off the transformation with a hint of her favorite cherry potion lip gloss.

She took a deep breath before she ran down the stairs. When she walked into the kitchen, conversation stopped dead. Her parents, and Paisley just stared at her.

Then her mother's face broke out into a grin. “Sweetheart you look…different!”

"Very different," her father said. "You haven't been using magic, have you?"

"I wish I could take credit for this but no, I asked Reed to do it."

"You do look different," Paisley said quietly. It was clear she was upset and trying not to show it.

"I just figured I'd try something new," Bexley said with relief in her voice. She figured she was lucky Paisley was still speaking to her. And it looked like she was going to keep quiet.

"Maybe I'll try it!" Paisley cried. She pushed her chair back and stood up.

Uh-oh, Bexley thought.

Mrs. Ireland put her hand on Paisley's arm. "There isn't enough time, honey."

"You're right. We'd better go," Paisley said. She gathered her books and started for the door.

Bexley threw down her napkin and ran after her sister. “Paisley, wait for me!”

Paisley stopped and waited, but she didn't say a word. Bexley kept up a steady flow of small talk as they walked along, even though her sister was barely listening.

They were almost at school when Paisley finally said, “Bex, why didn't you tell me you were going to do this?”

“Do what?” Bexley wore her most innocent expression.

“Please don't start, Bex. Why did you change the way you look?”

Bexley was squirming inside. Then it came to her. “I just decided Reed was right we're too old to dress alike.”

“But you could have warned me. We've been dressing alike since we were born. Why didn't you tell me?”

“It's really no big deal it was time for a change, that's all.” Bexley had noticed Sebastian Bradbury. Just wait until he saw the new Bexley Ireland.

Sebastian caught sight of the twins. “Hey, br—” he started to say, and then, “Heyyy.” He whistled after them.

Paisley flashed a disgusted look at her sister, but Bexley was in a different world, blushing and smiling at Sebastian.

“Bex, couldn't we—”

Before Paisley could say another word, Jett and Alexis ran up. “Bexley, you look gorgeous!” exclaimed Jett. The girls began talking excitedly. Paisley slipped away.

As soon as she was gone, Jett lowered her voice and said, “Audrey saw you walking to school. She says to tell you that you did a good job on all your pledge tasks. We’ll vote on you by the end of the week.”

“The end of the week!” Bexley moaned. “That’s practically forever! I don't know how I'll stand it!” But deep down she wasn't worried at all. She knew she would get what she wanted. Bexley Ireland was definitely going to be the next member of the Black Cats Club.

Five

In the girls' room on the first floor Paisley locked herself in one of the stalls and began to cry. She didn't understand it. It felt as though Bexley were moving on and leaving her behind. All of a sudden, she was going places without asking her along, and doing things without telling her about them. And now Bexley looked so different from her that no one could tell they were twins.

She heard the girls' room door swing open and choked back a sob. It was two sixth graders she didn't know very well.

"I've just got to do something with my hair," one was saying. Did you see Bexley Ireland? She must have had a makeover. She looks so much older. She doesn't even look like a twin anymore. It's amazing. I mean, now you know who's who."

“That's a relief,” the second girl said. “I wanted to get to know them better, but I was always afraid I start using the wrong name or something.”

The door slammed and Paisley was alone again. But now she knew exactly what she wanted to do she stood in front of the mirror. She undid her ponytail and let her hair fall free. Then she parted it in the middle, pulled it back from her face, and fastened it with a clip. It was a hairstyle she loved, and Bexley hated. She studied her reflection. She looked good, really good. Like a new Paisley Ireland.

After a last look she left, just as Olive Foster was coming in. “Hey, Paisley!” Olive’s eyes were wide. “You should wear your hair like that all the time.”

Paisley smiled. “Maybe I will,” she said.

And all day long, all over school, she heard the same thing. She looked great, Bexley looked great, and it was absolutely great that they had started wearing different clothes.

There was only one vote of disapproval. Mrs. Proctor sighed. “How sad it is that you and your sister aren't dressing alike! You used to look like two little dolls,” she said.

We probably did, Paisley thought. *Ugh.*

At dinner that night the family admired her new look too.

“Now I have two sophisticated little witches,” her father said.

“It's funny,” Paisley said. “I thought I would hate it, but I like looking different from Bex. I guess we won't be dressing alike anymore.”

“Thank the moon,” Reed muttered, while Bexley gasped, “never, ever?”

Paisley had to smile. “Maybe once in a while,” she said.

“Oh, good.” Bexley was relieved. “I still love us being twins. It's fun to dress alike.”

“Oh, girls,” Mrs. Ireland suddenly exclaimed. “I've got good news. I called Madame Pappenheimer’s School of Dance and a beginner's dance class is just starting tomorrow, in fact. It meets twice a week."

"Dance," Reed snorted. "Big deal."

But Bexley let out a shriek. "Oh, mom! Thanks!

Paisley was happy too. Looking different from Bexley was one thing but spending time away from each other would be something else entirely. She still wanted to be with her twin as much as she could. Now they could practice together—just as Paisley had hoped they would.

The next afternoon, the twins walked to the dance studio together. "I've been practicing so hard," Bexley exclaimed as she hurried Paisley along. "And look"—she held her dance bag open and pointed inside—"a new leotard."

Paisley pulled it out. "Black! What about your neon pink one?"

"Black is more sophisticated," Bexley said. "I borrowed black leg warmers from Jett. Maybe I'll dye my slippers too. I really want to stand out."

Mom will kill you if you dye your shoes!"

"Not if you don't tell her," Bexley said, and changed the subject. "Guess what, guess what? I caught Sebastian Bradbury looking at me today. I really think he likes me."

"I don't know what you see in him. He's a jerk and he's always picking on people.

They had reached the dance studio. As they pushed open the heavy glass doors, Bexley whispered, "I'm so excited!"

The receptionist was sitting at a large, overflowing desk just inside the entrance. She smiled as soon as she saw them. "Now, don't tell me. You're the Ireland twins. I'm Mrs. Howe."

She pulled out a clipboard and checked off their names. Go hurry and change and then go on into the studio. Most of the other girls are already inside. Madame Pappenheimer will be right with you. She waved towards the door.

Bexley squeezed her sister's hand. "Madame Pappenheimer! She is the head of the whole studio."

The dressing room was empty. “We'd better get moving,” Paisley said, aware that Bexley’s window shopping along the way had made them late.

Quickly she slipped into her neon pink leotard, gold tights, and green slippers. Pretty standard, she thought as she watched Bexley pull her black leotard from her tote bag.

Bexley was looking into the mirror and patting her hair, now back in a ballet braid. She had a little smile on her face. “I wonder...” she murmured. She noticed Paisley in the mirror behind her. “Oh, Paisley, you go ahead. It'll take me another minute to get ready. I want to look just right for Madame Pappenheimer”

“OK, slowpoke.” Paisley smiled. “But hurry up. Class is going to start any second.”

“I'll be right there.” Bexley waved her away.

Paisley went to the studio. It was a huge room, with mirrors lining two walls and the barre running along a third. About thirteen other girls were waiting for Madame

Pappenheimer. Paisley recognized just one of them—Puma Maddox from her potions class. They smiled at each other.

"Attention!" A whimsical voice with a French accent floated through the studio.

Paisley whirled around. A tall woman with gray hair flowing down her back was striding toward them. She held her head very high and had a huge smile on her face.

"I am Madame Pappenheimer. You can call me Madame Pappi," she went on sweetly. "Today we begin the study of dance. I will demand hard work from you, but you will enjoy the dance." Madame Pappenheimer held a long wand in her hand, and she wrapped the floor with it in time with her words, purple sparks flying from the end of the wand as it hit the dance floor emphasizing every word that came out of her mouth.

Paisley looked nervously toward the door to the dressing room. What on earth was keeping Bexley? Paisley was sure

Madame Pappenheimer expected all her students to be on time. And Bexley really wanted to impress her.

"Class, please face the front and sit on the floor while I call roll. "We begin." Madame Pappenheimer rapidly called out names from an alphabetical list in her hand, studying each face as a student raised their hand. Finally, she reached the I's. Bexley still hadn't appeared.

"Paisley Ireland?" She called. Paisley raised her hand. She was so nervous for Bexley, she thought she would faint.

"Bexley Ireland?"

"Here! I'm here!" Bexley appeared at the door to the studio. Now Paisley was positive she was going to faint. She couldn't believe her eyes.

"Miss Ireland!" barked the teacher.

"Yes?" Bexley said timidly.

"What is this costume? Do you think we were performing? First lesson, and you are a ballerina? In dance class we are eccentric and flowy. The dresses colorful. Do you understand? No black. No—none of this.” She crossed the room to Bexley, released the ballet braid, her hair cascaded over her shoulders. “We wear the hair down and flowing. It must not be stiff and stifle the dancing.

Paisley felt terrible. Poor Bexley! She was just trying to look professional and graceful. But Madame Pappenheimer was staring at her as though she were a monster.

Bexley’s face had turned white. It was true. Every other girl in the room was wearing their hair down and flowing.

Madame Pappenheimer handed Bexley a neon pink leotard. “Take off those things and fix your hair so you look like your sister.” She looked toward Paisley and nodded as though she was relieved that one Ireland was a proper dance student.

Her hands trembling, Bexley fluffed her hair.

“And next class,” the teacher continued, “be here before roll is called, like the others. And no black or dull colors.

Vibrant colors only—like your sister, and lots of makeup! Here we have no ballerinas, only dancers!"

Bexley nodded. She looked as if she wanted to cry.

As soon as Madame Pappenheimer turned her back, Paisley squeezed Bexley's hand. "Don't worry," she whispered. "It'll be OK."

"But it wasn't."

Bexley was too upset to concentrate. She did everything wrong during class. First, she mixed up the five positions, which Paisley knew she could do perfectly. Then she lost her balance during a spin dance and tripped.

"Très bien, Paisley! Very good, Puma!" Madame Pappenheimer kept saying. Or sometimes, "back straight, mademoiselle Maddox. Feet out!" But she didn't say a word to Bexley—not even when she tripped. She just looked at her coldly and called out. "Très bien, Beatrix!" to the littlest girl in the group.

When the hour was over and Madame Pappenheimer finally dismissed the class, Bexley turned to Paisley with her eyes full of tears. “I really messed up,” she said. “I ruined everything.” They walked in the dressing room together. “I can do all that stuff better than anyone else. She just made me so nervous.”

“I know.” Paisley put her arm around her sister. “You'll do better next class; Madame Pappi will forget all about today.”

Bexley sniffled. “I hope so.” But she was beginning to wish she had never taken dance. She had a feeling dance was going to be one huge mistake

“Paisley, why didn’t you tell me?” Lola Von Duren galloped across the cafeteria and practically tackled Paisley.

“Tell you what?” Paisley was totally puzzled.

“About your sister.”

Paisley gave Lola a blank look.

“And the Black Cats! Bex is so lucky! Hardly anyone gets to join the Black Cats.”

Join the Black Cats! Paisley’s stomach did a flip-flop.

Lola rattled on. “I heard she did a great job on her pledge tasks. It's just too bad they didn't have room for you, too.” Lola's eyes were glued to Paisley’s face.

Paisley wasn't listening anymore. “Yeah,” she said. “Look, I'm sorry. I've got to go now.” She walked out of the cafeteria as fast as she could.

She felt as though someone had knocked the wind out of her. Bexley joining the Black Cats! This had to be the biggest achievement in Bexley's life. And she hadn't told her about it—not a single word. Paisley's eyes filled with tears. Bexley would spend every free minute with the Black Cats now. And Paisley would be on the outside.

Suddenly she remembered that she and Bexley were supposed to walk to dance together right after school. For the first time in her life Paisley didn't want to be alone with her sister. Not now. Not the way she was feeling. She searched the halls frantically for someone who had a class with Bexley. There was Olive Foster—they had potions together. "Olive," she called, "could you tell Bex I can't walk to dance with her today?" Olive looked thrilled with the chance to do the favor.

"Sure!" She called back.

Somehow Paisley dragged herself through the afternoon. She dreaded the thought of facing Bexley. She just couldn't stand to ask her about the Black Cats, but somehow, she had to. When she reached the dance studio, Bexley was already there.

"Here I am," Bexley said cheerfully. "Miss Punctuality!" Then she looked at her sister. "Is something wrong?"

Paisley just shrugged and said, "not really."

"You look funny. You sure you're alright?"

Paisley nodded.

Bexley decided that this wasn't the time to worry about anything except dance. She just had to make up for Tuesday's lesson and impress Madame Pappi. She wore a green leotard like Paisley and had left her brown hair down. She thought she looked totally unsophisticated, but if that's what Madame Pappi wanted, that was what Bexley Ireland would give her.

Bexley made sure she was the first one in the studio, and when Madame Pappenheimer strode in with her dance slippers and wand, Bexley sat down before anyone else. She had positioned herself right in the front, so the teacher would notice her. She waited for Madame Pappi to acknowledge the change. But when she called Bexley's name—nothing! Madame Pappenheimer looked right through her.

The entire hour was the same. It was all "Bon Paisley! And "Très bien Paisley!" but for Bexley, nothing at all. By the end of the class Bexley felt absolutely invisible.

"Boy!" she said to Paisley in the dressing room. "I just can't believe this! And after all the trouble I went to. Wait until I tell the Black Cats—"

Paisley burst into tears.

"Paisley, what's wrong?" Bexley cried.

"Oh, Bexley!" Paisley choked as she grabbed her clothes and ran out of the dance studio.

Bexley stared after her. Suddenly she had the worst feeling. She just knew that Paisley had found out about the Black Cats Club. *But it wasn't my fault,* Bexley told herself. *I had to keep everything secret. And after all, I didn't try to upset Paisley. It just happened.*

“Mom, can I talk to you?” Paisley asked Mrs. Ireland as soon as her mother got home.

Mrs. Ireland was just hanging up her jacket and putting her bag away. She turned and saw her daughter's tear-stained face. “Oh, my little witch,” she said. “What happened?”

Paisley just shook her head. She couldn't speak.

“Let's go into the library,” her mother suggested. She closed the door behind them. She touched her wand to her daughter’s face and the tears where gone.

“Now,” she said, “can you tell me what's wrong?”

“Bexley is going to be a Black Cat,” Paisley burst out, “and she kept it a secret. She doesn't tell me anything. We never do anything together anymore. And she doesn't even care!” Paisley began to sob.

“Calm down,” her mother said soothingly. “Let's go back to the beginning. You said Bexley is a Black Cat?”

Paisley took a deep breath. “There's this club at school,” she explained. “The Black Cats Club. It's only for the girls who are pretty and popular. It's a really big deal. Only a few sixth graders get asked to join."

"Oh, thank goddess, I thought someone put a hex on Bexley," her mother said as she let out a sigh of relief. "Is it something you'd like? What does it club do?" Her mother asked.

"I don't know," Paisley sniffled. "Talk about boys, I think. Boys and clothes. Anyway, they didn't invite me."

"But my little smitch," her mother said, "that doesn't sound like something you'd enjoy. It sounds perfect for Bexley but not sophisticated enough for you," she said with a wink.

"Smitch?" Paisley asked. Their mother was always coming up with pet names to call them.

"Yes, smitch. My little smart witch," her mother said smiling.

Paisley wiped her eyes. "I guess I don't know if I'd want to be in it, but I still sort of wish they wanted me. Maybe it's really not the club. It's just that we used to do everything together, and now Bexley doesn't even want me around."

"I know that's not true," Mrs. Ireland said. "Twins can't be together all the time. It's good for you to do different things."

"Really?" exclaimed Paisley. "Bex and I should be apart?"

"Yes," her mother said gently. She hugged her daughter. You're growing up, that's all. And there's not a soul in the world who hasn't hit at least one rough spot growing up. Just remember—your father and I are here to help. You'll see. You'll find more and more things to do on your own."

"I guess so." Paisley sighed, but she still felt miserable. Her mother really didn't understand. She needed to spend *more* time with Bexley, not less. How could she let the Black Cats Club break them up?

Paisley found Bexley up in their room. She was sprawled in the bed touching her wand to each of her nails changing the color from orange to purple to pink back to orange. "You know you're not supposed to be doing magic. We'd better talk, Bex," she said

"Okay," Bexley said nervously. Besides the magic, she was almost sure she knew what Paisley wanted to talk about.

"I heard about you and the Black Cats Club today," Paisley began. "I felt really bad that you didn't tell me about it. But I guess you have a right to do things on your own. I'm trying not to let it bother me."

Bexley jumped up from the bed and threw her arms around Paisley. "Oh, Paisley," she cried. "Thanks for understanding."

"I talked to mom. She said it's good that we have separate interests."

"Oh, good. Paisley, I'm sorry. I wanted to tell you. I just didn't dare. All this pledge stuff is supposed to be secret. And I haven't even been voted in yet. I'm still scared I'll do something to ruin my chances."

“Don't worry. I know you’ll get in.” Paisley tried to make her voice cheerful, but in the pit of her stomach she felt the terrible emptiness. She was losing Bexley. What was she going to do without her twin?

Seven

The next morning was Friday. Bexley woke up even before the alarm went off. She was much too excited to sleep. It was probably the most important day of her life. She rolled over and saw her sister lying in bed, her eyes wide open. "Paisley! she said. "This is the day! The Black Cats are voting on me!"

"I know," Paisley said. She had a funny look in her eyes.

"What are you thinking about?"

Paisley smiled. "The old days. Remember the time we made a camp for our Morticia, and Gomez dolls out front, and his real tough kid came by and said he was going to wreck it, but you talked him into playing Adams Family with us?"

Bexley giggled. "Then his big brother came along and made fun of him, and he started pulling Gomez and Morticia's arms off. Then they ran off with Gomez." She stopped. "Did they give him back?"

"Gomez's probably sharing their jail cell." Paisley sighed. "I kind of miss stuff like that."

"Not me," Bexley said. "But I like remembering it."

"Maybe that's what I meant. But I am going to miss you."

"Am I going somewhere?"

"Well, sort of. Once you're in the Black Cats Club, we'll hardly see each other. Mom says we should do things separately, but I think it will be horrible."

"Hey!" cried Bexley. "I've got a great idea. If I get into the club, I'll get you in, too."

"Could you really? Then things could stay the same!"

"Sure," Bexley said. She knew the Black Cats thought Paisley wasn't right for the club, and she could see what they meant. But there had to be a way to get her in. Maybe it wouldn't be easy, but that had never stopped Bexley Ireland. She propped herself up on her elbows.

Just then the phone rang. Bexley made a mad dash for the phone in the upstairs office. She came back into the room a moment later looking shocked and closed the door.

"You will never in a million years guess who that was!"

"Who?"

"It was Katarina Black—for Reed. Reed must be the boy Katarina's in trouble over! I told her Reed was still sleeping." She smiled slightly.

"Hey, I wonder when Reed is going to get up." Bexley's face was full of mischief.

"Why?"

"Why? I want to talk to him about Katarina Black. For once we could get some gossip before Lola."

"But Bexley, he'll have a fit. And he's your own brother. Do you really want the whole school gossiping about Reed and Katarina? Don't forget, she was a Black Cat. That's not going to be a great for your image. The Black Cats sure won't like it—they just want people to know how popular they are, how gorgeous they are, and how perfect. Besides, didn't you say Katarina's boyfriend made fun of the Black Cats?"

Bexley clapped her hand over her mouth. "Oh, my gosh!" she cried. "I didn't think of that! Promise you won't say a single thing about it to anyone!" She acted as though Paisley had been planning to broadcast the news.

Paisley crossed her heart. "Not one word."

That afternoon Bexley threw open the kitchen door and shrieked, "I made it!! "I made it! I'm a Black Cat!

Paisley forgot all her feelings about the club. She leaped up from her seat at the kitchen table and gave Bexley a big hug.

"Oh, Bex! I'm so happy for you!" she cried.

"What's going on?" Reed came through the door.

"Reed!" exclaimed Bexley. "I'm a Black Cat! They voted me in this afternoon."

"A Black Cat in the family. Aren't we lucky? So, when do you get your tail?" Reed tossed his backpack on the floor and walked out of the room.

Bexley looked at Paisley. "Things must be rotten with Katarina."

"Let's just leave him—" Paisley stopped speaking when she saw Reed standing in the doorway.

"Just what was that crack?" The twins had never seen him so mad.

"Oh, nothing," Bexley said, backing away.

"You better remember this, both of you. Stay out of my business. I don't want to hear that name in this house," he said as he pointed his wand at the both of them. Then he was gone.

Paisley and Bexley stared at each other.

"Whew! What was that all about?" Bexley said.

"You got me, but I wouldn't mention Ka—her anymore. Let's forget about it. This is a happy day for you."

"It sure is!"

"Bex," Paisley asked, "how soon do you think you can try and get me into the club?"

Bexley had forgotten all about that. "I don't know," she said vaguely. "After a while."

Paisley seemed to wilt. She gave a big sigh.

Bexley had a load of potions homework that night and she wanted Paisley in a good mood.

"I just mean not in my first meeting," she said quickly. "But I can probably do it in my second!"

Paisley brightened right up. That wasn't long at all.

On Monday afternoon Bexley went to her first official meeting of the Black Cats Club. Paisley decided not to mope around. She invited Marissa Fairchild over. They had a lot to talk about anyway, and there never seemed to be time enough in school.

Paisley put her things on the kitchen table. “Do you want a snack? I like bologna and potato chip sandwiches, it’s ok if you think they’re gross. Bexley gags when she looks at one.”

“Well, I don’t think it’s gross.” Marissa started to giggle.

“You don’t?”

“No, I like bologna and pickles.”

“Bex would have you arrested.” Paisley laughed.

“I don’t tell many people,” Marissa said.

“Let’s eat outside,” Paisley suggested. “There’s this great place where I go all the time. It’s under an old weeping willow tree.”

“Wow, neat!” Marissa exclaimed when she saw it.

Paisley parted the branches. “It was our hideout when we were little. See, we made a bed of branches over there. This big root is the couch, and the branch that dips down is like a chair. This is where I write stories sometimes." She paused. "Bex never comes here anymore. She thinks it's babyish, I guess."

"Well, I don't. It's nice and private. We could have meetings about the magazine here. Top secret."

"Which reminds me," Paisley said. "We still have to come up with a name for the magazine."

Marissa groaned. "All my ideas are so blah—The Salem News, for instance."

"I know what you mean. What do you think of Hallway Chatter? It's Amaya's idea."

Both girls shook their heads. "Nooooo," they both said then they were quiet.

"Well, it should have something to do with magic in it," Marissa said.

"And something mysterious," Paisley added. she said slowly—and then it came to her. "Spells & Tells!"

Marissa looked amazed. "I love it. It's perfect."

"I didn't have any ideas before," Paisley said.

"You sure do now! There's just something about working with someone else, I guess." Suddenly Marissa's eyes lit up. "Why don't we try to write a book? I read about a kid our age who did it."

"A whole long book? About what?"

"Us. The kids at school. Real stuff."

Paisley was beginning to feel excited. "That would be wonderful. I haven't been doing much of anything, except the magazine. And dance."

Marissa frowned. "My mother keeps trying to get me to take dance. She hopes it will make me graceful and ladylike."

"My mother wants me to be more independent."

"Why can't our mothers just let us grow up by ourselves?" asked Marissa. "We're not stupid. We could do it. Hey, can I ask you something? How do you feel about Bex being in the Black Cats and not you?"

“Mostly—mixed up. I didn’t even like those girls before, but now—it’s just that the club will take up Bex’s time. What do you think of the Black Cats?”

“They are sort of…glamorous. But most of them have as much personality as a wet mop. All they can think about is what clothes to wear or who’s going to win the football game.” She looked at her watch. “Hey, it’s late! The time went so fast. I’d better go.”

After Marissa left, Paisley thought about the afternoon they had spent. It had really been great. It was too bad, though. Once Bexley got her into the Black Cats, she worried that she wouldn’t have time for her other friends anymore. But it would be worth it, wouldn’t it?

It was perfect. Bexley was at her third meeting of the Black Cats Club. She was actually sitting on Audrey Parker's white canopy bed. Jett and Alexis and all the other Black Cats were trying out different hairstyles and talking about Bexley's favorite topics—where to get the cutest clothes and how to get the cutest boys.

There was only one problem. Somehow Bexley had to figure out a way to get Paisley into the club—even though the Black Cats didn't really want her. Paisley was just not going to leave her alone until she kept her promise.

Finally, Bexley decided to come right out with it. At the first pause in the conversation, she clasped her hands together and said, "I have a suggestion, everybody."

"What is it?" Audrey asked.

"I think the Black Cats should take on one new member. She's really pretty and very smart—"

"Who is she?" asked Audrey.

"Paisley Ireland," Bexley said simply. She tried to look as though she expected everyone to start cheering.

"Your sister!" Audrey exploded. "Bexley, we talked about that already. We said Paisley wasn't right for us."

"Since I've become a member I've changed my mind," Bexley said as brightly as she could. "I think she'd be perfect."

"What a baby," snapped one of the eighth graders. "Can't you do anything without your sister? Come on, you're a big girl now."

It was time for a different approach. "Oh," Bexley said sadly. "Then I'll have to drop out of the club."

"What?" cried six girls all at once. "Why?"

Bexley made her voice waver slightly. "It's just that...well, my parents... they think that twins..." Slowly, Bexley began gathering her things together.

"Wait a second," Audrey said. She called the conference in the hallway with the two oldest members of the club. Two minutes later they were back.

"Look, Bexley, we don't want you to drop out. I mean, how would it look? It's OK for us to kick people out, but it's different for somebody to quit. So, we're going to give Paisley one pledge task, and it's not going to be an easy one"

"I'm sure she would do anything. Will you really give her a chance?" Bexley asked.

"Sure," Audrey said. "Ask her to sit with us at lunch and we'll tell her what the task is."

"Great!" Bexley exclaimed. That's all my parents can ask for—a chance.

To herself she added, *Bexley, you are a genius!*

As soon as Bexley got home, she told her sister the good news.

Paisley looked as if she had gotten a best present in the world. "Oh, Bexley," she cried. "This is wonderful! Now we can be together again!"

The very next day Bexley led Paisley to the Black Cats special table in the cafeteria.

Audrey got right down to business. "OK, Paisley," she began, "Bex probably told you we're thinking of letting you join the Black Cats. But before you can get in, you have to do a pledge task. If we like the way you handle it, we vote on you."

Paisley nodded.

"Of course, we're going to make it easy on you. Most girls get three tasks. We're giving you only one."

"That's fine with me," Paisley said.

"Here's what you have to do," Audrey went on. "Invite Olive Foster to go to Captain Dusty's with you after school on

Wednesday. Order two ice cream sundaes, and when they're ready, say you'll get them while Olive saves your table."

Paisley kept nodding. This didn't sound bad at all.

"Then, on your way back, scrape the whipped cream off Olives' sundae and cover it with this instead." Audrey reached into her bag on the table and pull out a can of shaving cream. "Can't you see her face when she gets a mouthful out this glop?"

"Make Olive eat shaving cream?" Paisley cried. "No way! I can't do that to someone. Especially not to Olive. Everyone is already so mean to her." Paisley stood up.

Bexley gasped. "Paisley!"

"Look, think it over." Audrey didn't look surprised at all. "It's your ticket into the club. Take it or leave it. Just let us know tomorrow."

Paisley left the table.

Behind her Bexley faced the rest of the girls. She was furious at her sister. “She'll do it,” she said. “Believe me, she'll do it.”

Paisley slumped down in the seat next to Marissa and Amaya.

“Wow,” Marissa whispered, awestruck. “They want you to join, don't they?”

“Yes,” Paisley said angrily. She wadded her lunch bag into a tight ball. She would never play such a rotten trick on Olive, or anyone else. Not in a million years.

The minute Bexley got home she marched straight to the weeping willow tree in the backyard. She was sure Paisley would be out there.

“How could you do that to me?” She cried. “You made me look like a fool. Do you know how hard it was to—to—Oh Paisley, you can't say no!”

“Bexley, I'm sorry. I really want to be in the club with you, but I won't do that to Olive.”

"You are such a goody two shoes. A real Glinda! A first-class goody two shoes witch!"

"You can call me whatever you want," Paisley said in a firm voice, "but there are some things I won't do, and hurting a kid like Olive is one of them."

"You're not going to poison her, it's not like it's Belladonna, it's shaving cream" Bexley objected. "She's just going to taste it."

"That's not what I meant. It would embarrass her."

Bexley rolled her eyes. "It's only a joke. It'll be funny. Everyone will laugh."

"At Olive. Bexley, I can't do it." Paisley turned her back. "That's the end of it."

"That's what you think!" Bexley snapped. Then she whirled and stalked into the house. There was no way Paisley was going to make a fool out of her. In another minute she was talking on the phone to Audrey Parker.

"OK," she said, her voice low. "Paisley changed her mind. She'll do it. And Wednesday will be fine." Bexley knew that her sister had a dentist appointment that day.

There was a shocked silence on the other end of the phone. Slowly Audrey said, "she'll really do it?"

"Sure. I can talk her into anything."

"Wednesday it is, then."

"Great," Bexley said. "Oh, but I won't be there. I've got a dentist appointment on Wednesday." She hung up the phone and immediately opened her laptop to check the Black Cats group chat. Just as she thought... Audrey had sent out a group text passing the word along. By the end of the evening every Black Cat in Salem would know that Paisley Ireland was going to make Olive Foster eat shaving cream. The plan was going to work!

Paisley's eyes were just fluttering open on Wednesday morning when Bexley put her plan to action. “Paisley,” she said, “you know what you should wear today? Your pink and white striped shirt and your white pants. You always look so good in that outfit.”

Paisley rubbed her eyes. “OK,” she mumbled sleepily. “Maybe I will.”

“You’ll look great,” Bexley said cheerfully.

So far, so good, she thought. This was the day when it was going to happen, when Paisley Ireland was going to do her pledge task. Only Paisley wasn't going to know a thing about it.

Bexley had set it all up the night before. She almost giggled when she thought about how she had called Olive and asked her to Captain Dusty's. She had done a perfect Paisley imitation. She was only sorry no one had been around to appreciate it.

First, she had put on her friendliest voice. Paisley would be nice to a hissing cockroach. "Hi, Olive, this is Paisley Ireland," she'd said.

"Paisley!" Olive was thrilled. "Hi, thanks for, I mean, how are you?"

Oh, brother, thought Bexley, but she had been Miss polite. "Oh, just fine, thank you. Listen, I was wondering if you'd like to get a sundae at Captain Dusty's after school tomorrow." She nearly choked on the words.

"Sure!" Olive exclaimed. "You bet! What time?"

Bexley could barely believe she was actually making a date with Olive Foster. "I'll meet you on the front steps after the last bell. OK?"

"Great! This will be so much fun!"

Fun! Bexley had thought as she hung up. Eating in public with Olive would be as much fun as having her head shaved. But she kept reminding herself, it wasn't going to hurt her image. Everyone would think she was Paisley, friend to the world.

So that day Bexley put on a neon pink dress, and Paisley wore the outfit Bexley had suggested. Bexley wore her hair down and Paisley wore hers pinned back. Paisley faced was free of makeup and Bexley carefully put on lip gloss, and a little mascara. The girls barely looked like twins.

After school Mrs. Ireland picked Paisley up right on schedule and started off for the dentist. Bexley watched from a second-floor window. The minute they were gone she dashed into the girl's room. she changed into her own pink and white striped shirt and white pants. Then she pinned her hair back, removed her plastic bracelets, and washed off the makeup. *There*, she said to herself. *Just like Paisley.*

Casually, Bexley walked into the hall and through the corridor to the front steps. Olive was already there.

"Hi Paisley," said Olive, awkwardly clamoring off the wall she been sitting on. "Thanks for asking me. It's so nice to do things with a friend."

Bexley cringed. Her pal. "Hi, Olive", she said with Paisley's nicest, friendliest smile. Then her mind went blank. What would Paisley do? What was she say? "How is history going?"

"History," Olive scoffed. She started talking and didn't stop until they reached Captain Dusty's.

Inside, Bexley glanced around and saw Audrey, Blair, Margot, and Jett sitting near an empty table. As soon as the Black Cats saw Olive, they began to turn red from trying not to laugh. Bexley quickly walked up to the counter, where she and Olive ordered hot fudge sundaes.

"With marshmallow cream," Olive added. "And nuts. And Cherry syrup. Oh, and toasted coconut."

Bexley nearly gagged at Olive's order, but she kept an angelic expression on her face.

"That will be about five minutes," said the man behind the counter.

"Let's go find a table," Bexley suggested.

She steered Olive to an empty one near the Black Cats.

While they waited for their order, Bexley tried to concentrate on acting like Paisley. Every once in a while, she thought Olive looked at her strangely. *Remember,* she kept telling herself, *you're quiet, calm, sincere, nice. You like school. You like potions. You like Olive.* She was starting to worry.

Then just then their order was called out. Bexley jumped up and looked around. "Gee, it's really crowded today," she said. "Why don't you hold our table? I'll go get the sundaes."

"OK," said Olive.

Bexley saw Jett grinning at the next table as she walked to the counter. Just as Bexley put the sundaes on a tray, Blair took her by the elbow and pulled her behind a column. She was holding a spoon and a can of shaving cream.

Bexley crouched down low and balance the tray on her knees. She took the spoon from Blair, scraped the whipped cream off Olive's sundae, and dumped it into a nearby trash can. Then she shook the can of shaving cream and squirted a huge amount on the sundae making peaks and swirls. Blair disappeared, and Bexley casually walked to her table.

"Here we go," she said brightly as she sat down. She set Olive's sundae in front of her.

Olive stared at it. Then she looked up at Bexley. "Hey," she said. She was frowning.

Bexley nearly fainted. Had Olive figured everything out? "What? What's wrong?" She asked nervously.

"They forgot the coconut."

Bexley trembled with relief. "It's probably underneath," she said shakily. She scooped the cherry on the top of her sundae and held in in front of her. "Cheers," she said.

Olive smiled happily. She took an enormous spoonful of cream, toasted Bexley’s raised spoon with it, and aimed it toward her mouth, her eyes closed in anticipation.

“Ew, ew! Ick! Yuck!” Olive spat the shaving cream into her napkin. “What is this? This isn't—" Olive stopped. At the next table Jett, Blair, Margot, and Audrey were laughing hysterically. Across from her, the girl she thought was Paisley was covering her mouth with a napkin and giggling.

“It's a joke!” Paisley cried, when she was able to talk again. “It's shaving cream!”

Olive’s lip began to quiver. “Paisley, how could you do this to me?” Her voice dropped to a whisper as her eyes filled with tears. “You are always nice to me. Now you're acting just like Bexley. I—I don't understand.” Very slowly, she stood up. Then she walked out of the Captain Dusty’s, crying silently. She didn't look back.

Audrey sat across from Bexley. "Well, you did it." She sounded surprised. "I have to admit, I didn't think you would, but you did. We'll let you know soon about the club."

The only way to prevent the Black Cats from finding out the truth would be to keep Paisley from discovering what she had done. So that night Bexley called Audrey, proposing that the Black Cats not congratulate Paisley on her pledge task until they were sure they wanted her in the club. "You know how hurt Paisley would be if you rejected her after all that she's gone through," Bexley was explaining to Audrey with a sympathetic tone.

Now Bexley was temporarily off the hook! At least until their first meeting. By then she was sure that she'd be able to handle her sister.

The next day Bexley went to her dance lesson feeling great. If she could fool Paisley, Olive, and all the Black Cats, how hard could it be to get Madame Pappi to see the truth that Bexley Ireland was a terrific dancer.

It didn't work out that way.

Bexley was dressed in a regulation neon pink leotard and Jett's purple leg warmers, which were purple with pink hearts and yellow stripes. Besides that, she had knotted a sheer hot pink scarf around her waist and untied her hair so that it tumbled over her shoulders in waves. The sides were pinned back with glittery barrettes. Long pink streamers dangled from the barrettes. Last, but definitely not least, she had smeared green eye shadow all the way up to her eyebrows. She was definitely the eccentric dancer! She was dancing really well. But, still, Madame Pappi never had anything nice to say to her. Toward the end of the class Bexley did a jump that she knew was much better than anyone else's. Madame Pappi looked right at her and said coolly, "Next time, higher." That did it.

In the changing room Bexley actually yanked off her dance slippers, pulled the skirt over her leotard, and stomped out.

Paisley gathered up her things and ran after her. “Hey, Bexley! What's the matter? Wait!”

Bexley was outside by the time Paisley caught up with her. “That does it! I quit.”

“You what?” Paisley cried. “Don't quit! Please. This is the only thing left that we do together.”

“Don't worry about that. You're getting into the Black Cats Club.”

“What are you talking about?”

Oops! How had she let that slip? Bexley had to think. “I have a feeling they'll change their minds. Because of me, I mean.”

Thanks, Bex, but I really doubt it. Anyway, I still don't think you should quit dance.”

Bexley was feeling a little calmer. “Neither do I, but Madame Pappi is totally unfair. She hates me. Why should I be tortured twice a week?”

“So, you're just going to let her get the better of you? Why don't you stand up to her? Get back at her.”

“Yeah, I guess staying in class would really teach her,” Bexley said sarcastically.

“Oh, you know what I mean,” Paisley said lightly. “Besides, it's not like you to give up.”

“I'm not giving up.”

“Aren't you? This is the only dance class in Salem. Once we stop dancing in gym, dance will be over for you. You’re letting Madame Pappi keep you from something you love.”

Bexley knew that was true.

“Why don't you try one more class?”

“Maybe,” Bexley said reluctantly.

“Bexley, please.” Paisley's voice rose slightly.

"OK, OK, OK. One more chance from Madame jump-higher, and that's it."

Bexley showed up to dance on Tuesday, almost sure it would be her last class. But something happened that changed her mind.

Just before the lesson ended, Madame Pappi called the girls around her and said, "I have a very important announcement. In two months, all of you will perform for the public." There was an excited murmur from the girls until Madame held up her hand. "Pappenheimers School of Dance will hold a recital on Gallows Hill for All Hallows Eve, and all of Nathaniel Hawthorne High will be there and most of Salem. Madame's eyes gleamed with excitement. "I have many times danced on the stage, and no experience can match it. This class will perform a lovely scene from the dance Adelaide. Do you know the story?"

The girls shook their heads.

“I will tell you then,” said Madame Pappenheimer. “Adelaide is a story of Mariposa, a beautiful witch who was in love with a handsome warlock named Felix. Mariposa is afraid that Felix loves Adelaide, a girl he has seen from afar in a Humbum village. Then she learns Adelaide is his half-sister and her dream of marrying Felix comes true. But before that, Mariposa and her friends dance in the meadow with the lovely whimsical butterflies, and this is the scene we will do. It has many charming parts. Then, of course, we need Mariposa herself. Her solo is very beautiful, but very difficult. A very good dancer is needed for that part.”

“I suggest you all practice hard. Soon I will hold auditions for the recital, and each of you will have your chance. Are there any questions?”

“What does Mariposa wear? Asked Bexley, thinking of flowy white gowns and silver crowns.

“Not black leotards,” snapped the teacher.

For heaven's sake, wouldn't she ever forget that? So, she had gotten off on the wrong foot, thought Bexley. There was still such a thing as forgiving and forgetting.

Right then and there Bexley promised herself to stick with Madam Pappi's class no matter what. She would practice hard. She would make Madame Pappi see how good she was, and she would win the part of Mariposa. When they performed Adelaide, Bexley Ireland would be the star.

Ten

That evening Bexley burst into the kitchen screaming Paisley's name. You're in the Black Cats Club! Jett just called. They held a special meeting to vote on you."

Paisley just stood there, absolutely amazed. Then she threw her arms around her sister. "Oh, Bex, that's wonderful! But what made them change their minds? I mean, how did I get in?"

Bexley was ready for this. "I told you. Because you're *my* sister. They want to keep me happy."

"You just joined, and they did this for you? They must really love them some Bexley Ireland."

"They do like me an awful lot," Bexley said modestly.

"I'm so glad they decided against that awful pledge task," Paisley went on. "They must have realized how much it would have hurt Olive's feelings. You know, Olive has been out of school for several days. She must be really sick or something."

"Must be," Bexley said. She was feeling a little nervous about Olive, suppose shaving cream was poisonous after all? *Oh, don't be silly*, she told herself. Anyhow, the Black Cats Club was the important thing.

"Oh, Paisley, don't make any plans for tomorrow. Black Cats always hold their meetings on Wednesdays."

"Great!" Paisley said. And she meant it. If Bexley liked the club so much, it had to be fun. Besides, the Black Cats must be pretty nice since they decided she didn't have to play that trick on Olive. And from now on she would be with Bexley all the time!

Bexley looked at Paisley's cheerful face and started congratulating herself all over again. Look how happy she had made her sister! Of course, there might be a few bad moments during the meeting if one of the girls said something about

Paisley's pledge task. Bexley put the thought aside. Probably nobody would. If the subject did come up, Bexley would change it fast. Anyway, Paisley had nothing to complain about. She hadn't done anything she didn't want to do, and she was *still* in the club. Bexley had done her a big favor.

The next day Paisley was sitting on the floor of Alexis Jacobs bedroom, surrounded by Black Cats. She had been there for forty-five minutes. She knew because she must have looked at her watch about twelve times. Everybody else seemed to be having a great time, but she was bored to death. This just couldn't be what the meetings were really like.

She looked around Alexis' room. She had never seen so many crescent moons in her life. They were on the walls, hanging from the ceiling, on her wastebasket. She even had them on her hairbrush and her laptop case. Maybe she should count them. That would help her stay awake.

"Attention, please!" Audrey called from Alexis' bed. Did everyone see the new Tom Holland movie last night?

The girls nodded their heads. Well, Paisley thought, they were going to discuss the movie. That could be interesting. Bexley had only gotten her to watch part of it, but Paisley had read the book.

"Isn't Tom cute?" Sighed Griselda Astor? One of the eighth graders.

"So hot," Margot said with her eyes half closed.

"I'd do anything to go out with him," Alexis said. Paisley felt as though her head were filling up with oatmeal.

"Did you hear he's going to be in a miniseries next month for four nights, The Lipnickies or something, Jett put in.

Paisley perked up. "That was a fantastic book!"

The other girls looked at her as though she were speaking Goblin.

Bexley quickly changed the subject. "Did you hear what Ophelia Tempest wore to the Bit Bar the other night? A bright red bra under a tight white t-shirt! You could see the whole thing!"

“She loves people to stare at her. She's as bad as Rosemary Humphries”

Paisley felt lost. She had never even heard of these kids they were talking about.

“That reminds me,” said Audrey, “I found out something we've all been wanting to know for weeks.”

Paisley straightened up a little.

I found out what size bra Elvira Murphy wears.”

Jett nearly shrieked. “What? What size?”

Audrey paused dramatically. “Are you ready for this? 36 E.”

There was a chorus of *wows*, but Paisley just stared into space.

“And you know who likes her?” Audrey went on.

“Every single boy in school?” Asked Bexley.

“Close. Zane Draven.”

“Zane Draven?” cooed Alexis. “He's so cute.”

Paisley thought, *if I hear "he's so cute" one more time, I think I'll throw up.* She checked her watch again and stifled a yawn.

Bexley poked her. How could her sister be so rude? She had hardly said one word during the whole meeting. How ungrateful! If she kept this up, having her in the club is going to be awful.

"Well," Jett was saying, "I don't know who my idea of a dream date is. Maybe Tom Holland. What about you, Paisley?

"Hmm?" Paisley tried to reel her mind in.

"Who would be your dream date?" Jett repeated.

Oh, brother, thought Bexley. This was going to be good. *Please don't say anything too weird*, she's silently begged her sister.

"Dream date? Paisley repeated. "Nobody, I guess. I'm not really interested in—"

"In any one person," Bexley finished hastily. "Right, Paisley? I mean, there are just so many. Paisley likes tons of guys. I'll tell you my dream date. It's Jax Morgan from *Toil and Trouble*."

"Oh, Jax Morgan!" Breathed Griselda. "He's so cute."

The meeting dragged on. Centuries seemed to pass before Audrey finally announced that the meeting was adjourned. "Let's go to the Bit Bar," she added.

As the girls stretched and began getting their things together, Alexis came over to Paisley. "I heard all about your pledge task!" She grinned.

Bexley turned pale. "Paisley," she said quickly. "How's the magazine going?"

But Alexis was rushing on.

"I just wish I could have been there. I would have loved to see Olive's face when she shoveled in that shaving cream. Listen, are you coming to the Bit Bar?"

Paisley was speechless. "No," she finally said, her mind racing. She knew instantly what must have happened: *Bexley* had done her pledge task. She had lied to her. She had impersonated her. Her own twin had betrayed her. “Bexley,” said Paisley, her voice shaking with anger, “I will never forgive you for as long as I live.” Paisley turned on her heel and walked out.

“Gosh. What's her problem?” said Alexis to Bexley.

“Beats me?” Bexley replied uncomfortably. “Come on let's go.”

Paisley had never been so angry. She walked into the house and slammed the kitchen door behind her. She thought she was going to be the only one home.

“Why are you home so early?” she asked when she saw her mother.

“I finished up early.” Mrs. Ireland stood back to get a good look at Paisley “What’s wrong?”

“Ugh, everything.” Paisley sighed.

“Sit here and talk to me while I start dinner.”

"Well," Paisley said slowly, "Bexley got me into the Black Cats Club."

"You don't look very happy about it."

"I went to my first meeting, and it was horrible. It was so boring, it literally felt like my brain was melting and then they asked me a question, and I said something really stupid. But mom, the worst thing is that they don't *do* anything. They just sit around and gossip. I hate everything about it." Of course, she wasn't going to tell her mother what really happened at the meeting.

Mrs. Ireland left the potatoes she was peeling and sat down next to her daughter. "My smart little witch, I'm not surprised."

"I had a feeling you wouldn't be. You said the club didn't sound right for me. I didn't want to listen."

"What I really meant was that you and Bexley may look alike, but you are two different very different people."

“I guess the club shows how different we are,” Paisley said thoughtfully. “But mom, I still feel like I'm losing Bexley.”

“Oh honey,” said Mrs. Ireland you may not spend as much time with Bexley as you used to, but you'll never lose her. She's your identical twin. Do you know how special that is?”

Paisley started to smile. “Yeah.”

“But even if you are a twin, you're also you. I think it's time for you to stop following Bexley, even if it's hard at first. “Do what you want to do. Try being on your own. After a while I think you're going to like it.”

On my own, thought Paisley. Well, she already had Marissa and Amaya and the magazine; *Spells & Tells*. Maybe she was starting to be on her own after all.

And as Paisley-on-her-own, there were a few things she had to straighten out.

Eleven

Paisley headed straight for the phone in her parents' bedroom. She was going to call Olive Foster right away, before another minute went by.

A woman answered the phone.

Paisley cleared her throat. “Is Olive there, please?”

“Who's calling?”

“It's... Paisley Ireland.”

There was a silence on the other end of the line. “I'm not sure she'll want to talk to you. Hold on.”

Paisley heard muffled voices and several bumps, as if the phone were being passed back and forth. Finally, Olive's voice came through the receiver. “Paisley?”

“Olive, I'm calling to explain and apologize—”

“Why did you do it? The other girls used to tease me, but never you.”

“Look, it wasn't me,” she said. “You know I wouldn't do something like that.”

“Oh, come on. I'm not blind.”

“Look, it was Bexley. It's a long story, but she was tricking those other girls into thinking she was me. Olive, I'm really sorry. I feel terrible.”

“I'm glad it wasn't you.” Some of the tension had left Olive’s voice. Then she added, “everyone was laughing at me. I thought I'd die.”

“I know. It’s a meanest thing I've ever heard of. I really hope you come back to school soon.”

“I can't go back.” Olive suddenly sounded tearful. “Not after that. It was too humiliating. We can't afford it, but my mom is looking into private schools.”

“Oh, come back, Olive, please,” pleaded Paisley. “You'll find kids like Bexley and Addison at any school. Why don't you sit with Marissa and Amaya and me at lunch tomorrow? We're starting an online magazine. Maybe you'll have some ideas."

"Well..." Olive said slowly. "Maybe. Thanks for calling, Paisley. I feel much better. I'll look for you tomorrow."

As Paisley hung up, she heard Bexley rummaging around in their bedroom. She marched right in.

Bexley sighed when she saw her. "Now, Paisley,"

"Don't," Paisley cut her off. "For once, Bexley Ireland you are going to listen to me. First of all, I want to say that I have never been so mad at anyone in my entire life. And you know what makes me maddest of all? Not what you did to Olive, even though it was awful and not that you lied to me about how I got into the club."

"But what, then?"

"That you thought it was perfectly fine to pretend you were me and let everyone think I would do such a thing. You acted as though I just don't count for anything."

"But you know I don't feel that way!" Bexley protested.

"Then you'd better start acting like it. I told Olive that I wasn't the one who did it. I want you to apologize to her."

"No way," exclaimed Bexley.

Paisley decided it was time she used Bexley's tactics on Bexley "I'm quitting the Black Cats Club, by the way."

Bexley didn't try to keep the relief out of her voice. "Well, I didn't think the club was exactly right for you."

"That is, I'm quitting if you apologize to Olive."

"I told you—" Bexley sounded very annoyed.

"If you don't do it, I might just stay in. As a loyal Black Cat, I'll have to tell Jett and Audrey and all the Black Cats everything—and I mean everything."

"This is blackmail Bexley shrieked.

"You should really apologize in person," Paisley went on as though Bexley hadn't said a thing.

"I won't!"

"Mom might be interested in all this too."

"All right. I'll do it. Are you satisfied?"

"Yes. Thank you. You've got exactly a week to apologize." Paisley turned to her homework without saying another word.

Exactly one-week later Paisley sat with Olive Foster on the wall by the front steps of Young Goodman Brown Middle School.

"I can't believe how much everyone liked the magazine," Paisley exclaimed happily. "I can't wait for my parents to read it."

"Hey, Paisley, *Spells & Tells* is great," Jett Andrews came down the steps of carrying her book bag. "I really like Lola's gossip column. How does she find out all that stuff?"

"I'm not sure," Paisley said with a smile, "but I'm glad you like it."

"The other Black Cats like the magazine too. When's the next edition coming out?"

"In a couple of weeks, I hope."

"Great! See you," Jett ran across the lawn to Alexis Jacobs, then turned around and yelled "Hey Olive, are you working on the magazine, too?"

"Not yet," Olive answered.

"Why not, you could do a fashion column and call it "What Not to Wear." Jett and Alexis burst out laughing and walked on.

"Jerks," Olive said. "I *really don't like* them."

"They're not my favorite people. Someone should give them a taste of their own medicine sometime," Paisley thought aloud.

"Hey," said Olive. "How come you asked me to meet you here anyway?"

"You'll see," replied Paisley. Just then Bexley appeared at the door and walked slowly down the steps. "Hi Olive," she said uncomfortably.

Olive stared down at the ground. "Hi."

"Um, Olive," Bexley began, her face reddening. "I want to tell you that I'm sorry about what happened at Captain Dusty's. I guess it was sort of mean."

"It was very mean," Olive said vehemently jerking her head up to look at Bexley.

"I know I hurt your feelings. So, I'm sorry." She paused. "You don't have to forgive me. I just wanted to apologize."

"Thanks, Bexley," Olive said quietly. "I'm glad you did." She looked up. "Paisley see you at lunch tomorrow?"

"Sure. We'll talk more about the magazine."

Olive hurried toward the waiting school bus.

"I know you didn't want to do that," Paisley said to Bexley, "but it meant a lot to Olive. And to me."

"It's just too bad she can't take a joke."

Paisley gave her sister a look. "Anyway, I won't tell her it was a pledge task, and I won't give you away to the Black Cats, if you never ask me to do your homework again."

“Alright...” Bexley’s voice trailed off. A moment later her emerald-green eyes were sparkling again. “Hey, I meant to tell you. The magazine was great. Everyone was talking about it. Maybe I should work on it.”

Paisley had to smile. She had been dying for this to happen, and now it didn't seem important. “I wouldn't say no, but are you really, really sure you want to?”

Bexley grinned. “Well, if you put it that way... I'm still awfully busy.”

Twelve

"For heaven's sake, what is going on here?" Mrs. Ireland was standing in the doorway to the twin's room. They had been shouting at each other so loudly neither one had heard her calling. "In exactly five more minutes you are going to be late for school."

"Mom. Bexley is a slob," Paisley snapped.

"Paisley that's a terrible thing to say," exclaimed her mother.

"Well, she is a slob. She spilled potion pop on my desk and look at her side of the room."

Her mother stared at the litter of clothing, paper, crumbs, and makeup and murmured, "terrible, but accurate."

"My half wouldn't be so messy if you weren't crowding me out. And besides if we could use magic, I could have this cleaned up in no time" Bexley told her twin.

"Alright! We don't have time to discuss this now," said Mrs. Ireland. "We'll talk about it tonight."

Over dessert that evening Mr. Ireland grinned at the twins and said, "get ready, girls. We have some big news. You're each going to have your own room."

"Our own rooms," shrieked both girls simultaneously.

"That's right." Mrs. Ireland laughed. "I just never thought about it until this morning. All we have to do is turn the guest room down the hall into a bedroom."

Then I'll never have to live in a messy room again," Paisley looked ecstatic.

"And I can be just as messy as I like," Bexley said with a satisfied smile.

"I don't think that's the idea, Bex," Reed remarked, but he was smiling more cheerfully than he had in a long time.

“We can redecorate, too,” Mrs. Ireland went on. Bexley you can stick to pink and white if you want it's up to you. Paisley you'll probably want something entirely different.”

“I want aqua blue curtains.” Paisley said smiling. “And plain white walls and a gigantic desk, with lots of drawers for paper and quills and a wall of bookshelves for my books. I just can't wait.”

Then, Mr. Ireland told her, “We’ll try to get it all finished this weekend.”

After dinner Paisley and Bexley went up to their room.

“Maybe by next week we won't be roommates anymore,” Bexley said. “You know, even after all the fighting we've been doing, I'll kind of miss sharing everything with you.”

“You will?”

“Sure. We've shared a room all our lives. I'll miss lying in a bed at night talking.”

“Me too,” Paisley sighed. But, Bexley added, “I won't miss your ten million books.”

“And I won't miss your pile of clothes.”

“Or all your lectures on neatness.”

“Or your candy wrappers in my bed or the crumbs on...” Paisley grinned.

“You better cut this out before we start fighting again.”

“I know,” exclaimed Bexley as she leapt up from her bed. “Let's go practice dance. The auditions are coming up really soon.”

“I don't think I will.” Paisley looked toward her night table. “I've got a new book of poems I want to read.”

“You can read that anytime!”

Paisley smiled at her sister. “I want to tell you something. A couple of weeks ago I would have said yes even though I didn't feel like practicing, which I don't, just so we would be together. But now I don't have to stick to you like glue. I can do what I really want to.” Bexley looked astounded.

"You mean you didn't before? I sure always do what I want!"

"Well, that was the trouble. So did I, always do what you wanted. I mean, but not anymore."

Bexley raised eyebrow. "I'm not sure I'm going to like this," she said but her green eyes were twinkling. If she really tried, Bexley was sure she would still be able to get her way with Paisley. Right now, it wasn't important, so she headed for the door. See you later, big sister. As Bexley left the room, Paisley gave a contented sigh, laid back on her bed and picked up her book.

The Irelands spent the entire weekend fixing up the twins' rooms. Everyone pitched in. On Sunday Reed and the girls were painting their guest room white for Paisley. Reed kept humming and sloshing paint on the wall in time to whatever he was listening to on his air pods.

"You've been in a good mood lately," Bexley remarked.

Reed winked at her. "Really?"

"Yeah, lost your fangs and everything. So, what was going on with you? Is it safe to ask now?"

Paisley stopped painting. "Katarina Black dumped you?"

"Why?" Bexley gasped. "Because you're older?"

"Well," Reed said, looking uncomfortable, "not exactly."

"Why, then? Come on, tell," Bexley coaxed.

"Ok, it doesn't really bother me anymore. But I don't want you kidding me about it and don't spread it around." He grinned sheepishly. "She said I was too immature."

"Oh, no!" Bexley shrieked and started to giggle.

"What does she want? An old man?" Paisley cried.

"I think she has a crush on some college kid—not that he's interested in her," Reed said. "It was pretty hard to take, especially with the high school kids saying I was a nerd for dating a baby. Anyhow, it's fine now." Reed cleared his throat "See, there's this other girl—a sophomore—"

"Oh, an older woman!" squealed Bexley. "That'll show Katarina."

"And this sophomore doesn't think you're so immature?" Paisley smiled.

"Oh, no. Not Livia," Reed answered. He raised his eyebrows. "We sit next to each other in biology. We're going to dissect dead things together."

Bexley wrinkled her nose. "How romantic," she said. She had started painting again.

"You know," Paisley said thoughtfully, "maybe Katarina didn't really mean what she said. Maybe she was just upset for getting grounded and kicked out of the Black Cats club and all."

"What do you mean kicked out?" Reed asked. "She dropped out."

Bexley nearly dropped her paintbrush.

"She got really annoyed after Audrey Parker asked me to go to a party with her," Reed went on. "And she quit."

Bexley's mouth dropped open, and Paisley started to laugh.

"Then—then," Bexley gasped, "here I was keeping it quiet, and Audrey knew all along you were the boy Katarina was seeing. She never said a word to me about you."

"What could she say? I just told her to wait and look me up when she gets to high school. I'm not going to make a hobby of dating eighth-grade girls.

Bexley eyed Reed with new respect. "So, the Black Cats—the most popular girls in school—were practically fighting over my brother!"

"Yep." Reed bowed. "Those Black Cats have great taste in men."

"Maybe so, but they're not very nice," Paisley couldn't resist bringing this up. "I mean picking on Olive Foster…how mean can you get? I wonder how they would like it if everyone laughed at them."

Bexley raised her eyebrows. “It’s silly even to talk about it. That could just never happen.”

“Well, somebody should show them—Paisley stopped speaking as, in a flash, it came to her. A brilliant idea. She turned her head away from Bexley and tried to smother the laugh that was bubbling up. Somebody would show them. Paisley Ireland!

Thirteen

The first chance she had, Paisley slipped into her parents' bedroom and shut the door. Then she dialed Olive Foster's number.

"Olive," she said softly, "how would you like to play a trick on the Black Cats?"

"I'm dying to get back at them. What do you have in mind?"

"I have a great idea. Listen to this. Tomorrow afternoon you and Marissa and I follow the Black Cats to Captain Dusty's. You act like you're by yourself, while Marissa and I get a table near the Black Cats. Then you go over and really make up to them, like you're sorry you got upset about the trick they played."

Paisley lowered her voice to a whisper and told Olive the rest of the plan. "So, what do you think?" she said when she was done.

"Perfect! I think you're a genius!"

The next afternoon Paisley and Marissa sauntered into Captain Dusty's, with Olive a few steps behind. "Over there," Paisley muttered to Olive. Six members of the Black Cats club—Bexley, Audrey, Jett, Alexis, Blair, and Margot—were already sitting at a booth waiting for their order.

Olive walked over to the ice cream display case, Paisley sat down, and Marissa put in their order in. Paisley saw Jett whisper something to Alexis and point to Olive. Knowing Jett, it was something really mean, thought Paisley.

Paisley glanced at Olive, who still seemed to be pouring over the ice cream selection and gave her the thumbs-up sign.

Olive acted as if she had just spotted the Black Cats. "Hi! I just wanted you guys to know I've been thinking it over and that trick you played on me was pretty funny. I mean, I know the Black Cats like girls to be good sports and all…"

Jett rolled her eyes. "Oh, you're such a good sport maybe we should consider you for membership?"

As the other girls started snicker, Order Eighteen was called out.

Jett stood up.

"Oh, I'll get your order!" Olive gushed. "You don't have to do that."

Jett smirked at the rest of the girls. "Oh, hey, sure, Olive. Why not?"

"Number eighteen!" the man at the counter called again.

"That's us, Jett. You'd better hurry," Olive said.

"You're on!" Paisley whispered to Marissa. Then she got up and followed Jett.

Marissa pulled a camera out of her tote bag and headed for the Black Cats table.

“How about a picture for *Spells & Tells*?” she asked. All the girls at the table turned on dazzling smiles just as though Marissa had turned on a switch. “Beautiful! Just a couple more,” she cried.

While Marissa was flashing away, Paisley pulled Olive, tray and all, behind a column.

“Three shakes, two hot fudge sundaes, and Jett’s strawberry sundae with chocolate ice cream,” Olive reported.

“Go ahead,” Paisley grinned. She held the tray while Olive spooned whipped cream off Jett’s sundae and piled it high with shaving cream. “Now let me get back to our booth before you take the tray to the girls.” Paisley hid the can of shaving cream in her book bag. Then she went back to the booth and waited while Olive stood at Bexley’s’ table, passing out the shakes and sundaes. When Olive had served everyone, Paisley strolled over to the Black Cats. “Hi, guys,” she said.

“Paisley!” Bexley squealed. She sounded more embarrassed than glad.

"Hi," muttered Audrey.

Jett dipped her spoon into her sundae and raised it to her mouth.

"Hey!" Paisley cried. "I wouldn't, you guys. I think that…she' Paisley nodded toward Olive, who was returning the tray—" might try to get back at you."

"Oh, come on, Paisley," said Jett. "Olive wouldn't have the nerve to do anything like that to one of us."

"I don't know," Paisley replied slowly. "I wouldn't let her get my sundae."

"Well, I'm not worried," said Bexley. She put a mouthful of whipped cream on her spoon and tasted it. "See? It's fine."

"So's mine," said Alexis, licking her lips.

"And mine," said Margot.

"And mine," said Audrey and Blair.

"And m—" Jett started to say but choked and spat out a mouthful of shaving cream. She stood up, gasping and gagging. Her eyes were closed, her face was screwed up, and her tongue was sticking out. "Oh! That was foul! Get me water. Who's got water? Anything?" She grabbed Alexis' vanilla shake and took a long swallow.

"Don't get any shaving cream in it!" Alexis cried.

"Oh, shut up!"

Jett suddenly noticed Marissa had appeared with her camera and was clicking away.

"Stop that!" she shrieked.

Everyone in Captain Dusty's was roaring with laughter, even the men behind the counter. Paisley and Marissa giggled so hard; they couldn't talk. The only ones not laughing were the girls in the Black Cats Club. Jett was a brilliant shade of red.

Paisley tried to get herself under control, but she and Marissa and Olive were practically falling over.

"I can't believe it!" exclaimed Audrey.

"This has never happened to the Black Cats," wailed Margot. "She made us look like fools."

"Come on, let's go." Audrey stood up. She headed for the door, with the other Black cats straggling along behind her.

"Good riddance!" Olive called after them.

The Black Cats ignored her as they rushed to the door.

Olive turned back to Paisley. "I did it! I really did it!" she cried. "I made fools of the Black Cats!" Olive Foster strikes back!"

Fourteen

One afternoon, two weeks later, Paisley was lying on her bed admiring her new room. It felt good just to be there. She had picked out a light grey carpet to go with the white walls, her curtains were aqua blue, and she probably had the biggest desk in Salem.

There was a knock on the door and Reed poked his head in. "Hey, why's the door shut?"

"I'm just enjoying my room." Paisley smiled. "Have you and Livia dissected dead things yet?"

"Yeah, yesterday. It was wonderful. My hand brushed Livia's as we both reached for the same scalpel. Then our eyes met over the—"

"Stop!" shrieked Paisley. "I don't want to know what your eyes met over. I'm sure it was gross."

"Wait until tomorrow." Reed put his hand over his heart. "We dissect a sheep's eye."

"Some romance." Paisley laughed. "But everything's going well for you, isn't it?"

Reed nodded cheerfully.

"For me, too. The Black Cats never figured out that the trick we played on Jett was really my idea. They were so relieved I didn't run those pictures in *Spells & Tells*—which I never intended to do—they just stopped mentioning the whole thing. It's lucky Lola Van Doren didn't find out about it or—oh, gosh, it's almost time to leave for dance. I'd better get Bex."

Reed waved and she hurried downstairs. A few minutes later she and Bexley were headed toward the dance studio.

"Should we take the shortcut?" Paisley asked.

"And go by the Good house? No way. Everybody says Mrs. Good's a wicked witch and the place is haunted."

"The place is creepy, but she can't be a wicked witch." Paisley glanced at her watch. "I guess we have enough time to go the regular way. I just don't want to be late."

"You don't want to. Imagine how I feel! I'm trying to get Madame Pappi to like me."

Someone whizzed by on a bicycle. "Hi, Bexley!" called a male voice.

"That was Sebastian Bradbury!" exclaimed Bexley.

"Nice of him to say hi to me," muttered Paisley.

"Oh, come one. He doesn't know you. Besides, did you notice what he called me?"

"Yeah, your name."

"Exactly. No more "brownie." Everybody's starting to see we really are two different people. We're the new Bexley Ireland and the new Paisley Ireland."

"That's right. The old Bexley was never interested in boys!"

"But the old Paisley would never have pulled a trick like the one you pulled on Jett." Bexley smiled slightly. "I was really mad when you told me you thought that up. I felt so humiliated when everyone in Captain Dusty's laughed at us."

"About the same way Olive felt when everybody laughed at her?"

Bexley made a face. "Ok. Anyway, you may be a goody-goody Glinda, but underneath it all, you're OK."

"Thanks a lot! I guess that's supposed to be a compliment. And you may be a wicked-wicked Elphaba, but I like you just the way you are."

Bexley laughed. "What I mean is maybe we don't agree on a lot of things, but you're my best friend."

"And you're mine!" Paisley was really glad Bexley had come right out and said it.

"That's the best part of being a twin…we were born with a best friend. We are the luckiest witches in Salem."

When the twins reached the dance studio Paisley was surprised to see Marissa standing glumly by her mother at the reception desk.

"What are you doing here?" she asked.

Marissa sighed. "My mother's going through with it. She's actually signing me up for dance."

"Come on, sweetheart," her mother said, smoothing back Marissa's hair. "You'll love it."

"Wanna bet?" muttered Marissa.

Paisley left her looking as though she were going to be executed.

"Saut de Chat! Cat's jump! Good, class! Paisley, very nice. Bexley, keep your back straight. And one, two, three, four. Good, class, stop."

Bexley leaned over to catch her breath. Madame Pappenheimer had given them a real workout.

“Now,” said Madame. “The auditions are close now. You must be in very good shape for them. And remember that you must work very hard to earn the part of Mariposa. Comprenez? Do you understand?” She smiled at Paisley.

Bexley’s stomach turned to ice. What good was it to be the best dancer in the class if Madame Pappi never noticed?

“Bien. Class is dismissed,” said the teacher.

The girls hurried to the changing room, but Bexley stood where she was, unable to move. She was beyond thinking about giving up dance. She had made up her mind. She just had to dance the part of Mariposa, no matter what. But what could she do to make it happen?

About the Author

J.L. Darling is a fantasy children's and YA author who is new on the scene. Her first book "Which Witch is Which" is the first book in the Sisters of Salem series. Born and raised in New England, she is a Rhody Girl through and through. She currently lives in Rhode Island with her Goldendoodle, Winnie. She is passionate about Dels Lemonade, Iggy's clam cakes, coffee syrup, Narragansett Beach, basically all things Lil' Rhody. When she's not writing she is going on adventures, walking the beach, dancing, eating ethnic food or drinking sangria. She is obsessed with all things magical i.e., babies laughing, rainbows, all animals, snow, shooting stars, and kisses from "The One."

Made in United States
North Haven, CT
12 June 2023